Dr. JOHN "SATCHMO" M

The Pearls of Love

POEMS AND STORIES FROM THE LAND OF NOD

ALADDIN BOOKS INTERNATIONAL INC.
A division of Lost Lamp Publications
P.O. Box 20478, New York, NY 10021
aladdinbooks@yahoo.com

Paperback ISBN:978-0-578-24552-2
Hardback ISBN: 978-0-578-24556-0

PRINTED IN THE UNITED STATES OF AMERICA

This Book of

LOVE

is a Gift....

From: _____

For: _____

On: _____

Occasion: _____

_____

_____

Dedication

With the name of G-D, the BENEFICENT, THE MERCIFUL....

This book is dedicated to all who have loved, to all who love; and to all who will love. By the token of time, by the pen, and by the starry night. I surrender that which was given to me, knowing that it belongs to you. I am only the carrier pigeon of a dream; one of many streams searching for the river of wisdom and the oceans of love, peace and understanding. If you are in love, I pray that you will love this book. If you are not in love, I pray that you will fall in love soon.... like the falling of the moon into the arms of the night!

THE PEARLS OF LOVE

Poems and Stories from the Land of Nod

(a.k.a. "Trading Treasures of the Heart")

Dr. John "Satchmo" Mannan

"Oh Wisdom, these words are the lamps that led me to your kiss."

Contents

THE FOREWORD
THE WAY OF THE PEARL

THE POEMS

The pearl is the most brilliant and sublime of all crystalline stones known to man. It has been prized for over six millennia by dozens of civilizations for its stupendous beauty and enduring symbolism. The pearl has symbolized to many the ever-evolving wisdom of the human mind and the kingdom of love that develops and dwells in the unselfish human heart. The pearl symbolizes these wonderful gifts because the pearl is the only precious gem whose beauty grows out of the acute striving, silent suffering and abundant hope of a living creature.

The pearl is the product of a living creature's effort to understand synthesize and harmonize the aspirations of a grain of sand-like substance who seeks shelter in a shell from the tempestuous currents and crosscurrents of life. Because of this striving and struggle (blues, if you will) in a living creature, the beauty of Pearl, is born. Thus, the pearl comes to symbolize a heavenly birth or the paradisiacal ending of a good man's journey through the vicissitudes of life and "outrageous fortune."

In the Bible, (where the Pearl is mentioned 10 times) The Kingdom of Heaven is described as "A PEARL OF GREAT PRICE" (Matthew 13:45 etc.) that the human soul must strive vigorously to attain.

Likewise, in the Quran (for example HQ 22:23 and HQ 52:24) "The Pearl" is mentioned various times in connection with souls who "believe in God and who do righteous deeds "dwelling in paradise and being adorned therein with bracelets of gold and pearl and their garments therein will be silk."

The consistency between the descriptions of pearls in these scriptures is like a seamless garment (adorned with stars) woven on the same loom. This is the way of the pearl as described in most earthly books of wisdom and heavenly books of understanding.

The Pearl in the foregoing contexts represents the pearl of wisdom and its subtle shine on one hand while also representing the Pearl of Love and its luminescent luster on the other. Love has the luster of patience and the endurance and commitment of patience. In youthful manifestation, love encounters and pursues passion, and then as time goes drifting by compassion grows.

Finally, love enters a rhapsody (-a third and final stage) which subsumes passion and compassion. Rhapsody is like a spiritual butterfly, who remembers that he was once a cocoon. So soon the seed has flowered a tree will tower above us Then the bluebird lingers no longer and soon enough the bluebird must fly also to the greater garden of pearls and flowers.

The poems and "stoems" (short story -poems) within these pages are the musings of "Poems Who Think" and who seek to explore the various dimensions of love from romance to remembrance from unrequited love to love which paces between the brain and the heart. The love between suitors and the objects of their affections are explored. The love between husbands and wives, between the sea and the sky between reasons and questions, "why'" mother and child, the musician and his art, between rubies and pearls, queens and kings and sundry wonderful things such as lilies and butterflies and purple mountains who embrace the sky are all explored in these pages.

THE STORIES

The Stories from the "LAND OF NOD, " in this book are a continuation of a line of parables, myths, and bedtime stories from my immediate preceding book: *"Mubassa's Drean"* and *"18 Legends from the Land of Nod."*

They are best when read at night, as they cross over from *The Land of Wakefulness*. You will have to catch a dream bus, a dream flight or the A train of thought which leaves from The Peoples Republic of Harlem, daily, Round Midnight. Check out "Dreamistan," "The Forest of Feeling," "The Mountain of Love," "The Wall Who Fell in Love," etc

Please keep an open mind and follow the *thinking instruments* given in stories for a smoother journey to and through Nod.

For your safety, if a character named "Sheik Sabir" from my previous book approaches you, don't give him the time of day. He will rob your imagination blind. He claims to be an incarnation of William Shakespeare, the ghostwriter of Othello, Hamlet, Romeo and Juliet, etc. Sheik Sabir is *Much Ado About Nothing*. So don't pay him any mind. I do confess that he is not a bad writer, maybe better than I.

THE SHELL *(the world within)*

Love, I have found, is a commitment. Man means mind. Man is as he thinks and dreams, learns, loves, and aspires. The body serves man both as a house and as a horse or modality of transportation by which the mind may travel around! Some minds always confine themselves to "the House." Others travel on wings to the celestial regions of the heart and other places and things. Even so the world begins with the art of love and life itself begins with divine love and a journey in search of love.

My work begins in contemplation of a great truth. This universe is a mental place and a mental space. I am but one mind, one-star woven in the tapestry of a mysterious and mystic curtain. It is this curtain that rises and descends upon the stage of a scripted play. I am a player given a choice within that script to play the part of a king or a fool.

In my previous form, I heard the call of a most beautiful singer in the night across a triple dark sea. I jumped in this dark deep sea along with over a billion other suitors who also heard this transforming call. I swam with all my might into the night ramming and slamming any other suitor who got in my way. I reached her first, I took her in my arms as she took me in hers. So, I was hers and she was mine. And we both built a dream house together East of the heart and West of our imaginations. So, three…"Me, Myself and I were born from our union.

Most human love lives and dies in a shell and the great pearl of unselfish love is never discovered.

My work herein begins with my contemplation and search for unselfish love. I searched for it within myself and in others as well. Whenever I find it, it is a pearl of great truth. I have grasped this unselfishness from time to time. Whenever I approached unselfishness, my hands are shaking like the wind-shaken leaves of autumn. They shake because I realized how small I am compared to a single leaf on the tree of life. So sometimes the pearl has eluded me. Love is an unselfish commitment. This truth has humbled and elevated me all at once.

In this book are the experiences of a heart.

A heart who has fallen when taking infant steps, a heart who now walks on the water of understanding carrying the staff of experience. Experience is not always wisdom but sometimes wisdom disguises herself as experience and sometimes experience disguises himself as wisdom. The scale that weighs hearts determines the destiny of love on earth and heaven. What is weighed on earth is weighed in heaven.

I share here what I have discovered. I have lived. I have loved. I have lingered.

Dear reader, these are the pearls of love. They are the scattered children of my heart and mind. If they do not engage you, it is because my journey is not over; and I have not trained them well. Sometimes Hydrogen marries Oxygen, but the impetuous couple does not always produce or hold sweet water. And so we thirst for wisdom.

Please read and travel. Read and enjoy our excursion to **THE PEARLS OF LOVE** and **THE LAND OF NOD** up above. Dine in our restaurants and cafes where we serve delicious scallops and scattered pearls *LOVE ALWAYS,*

Dr. John Satchmo Mannan

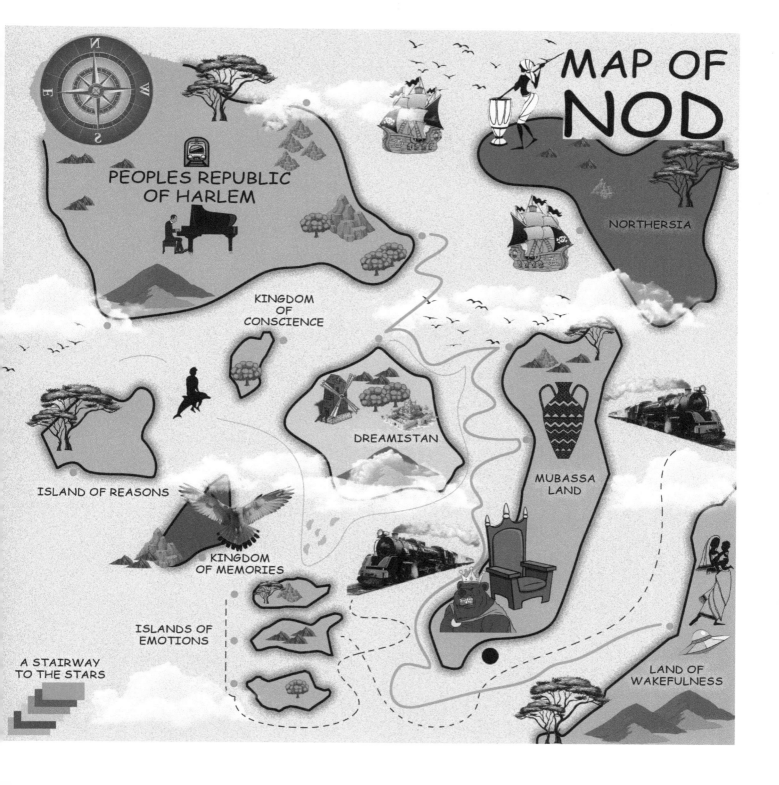

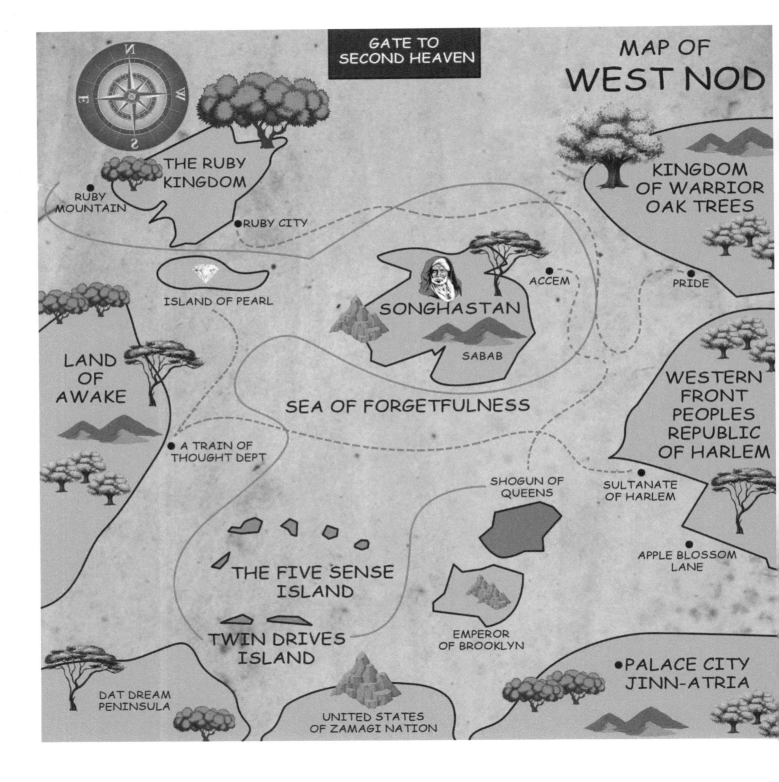

Acknowledgements

I am indebted to many that have helped me with this book, which I started writing during the US coronavirus lockdown. It was a time of tragedy and insanity for all of humanity. In the fog of insanity and despair, I witnessed thousands of points of light via random acts of kindness. People made masks and prepared food for front line workers. People gathered food for distribution to the hungry and homeless. The distressed gave comfort to each other. These acts of kindness were kindled by deep reservoirs of human love that dwells deep beneath the streets of our mundane modern lives.

The worldwide reaction to the death of George Floyd made us one human family of empathy and love for a brief shining moment; and made us all confess that what unites us humans is the true spirit of love. It took these tragic circumstances to make me think about writing about the key dimensions of the human love experience.

First, I acknowledge the Creator Who gave me inspiration and motivation to write this book to serve Him by serving humanity. Next, I would like to thank Lillian J. Jones, who read, critiqued, and shared her considerable insights on every piece of literature and art in this book. Her trustworthy insight was invaluable. Also, I am grateful for the wisdom and artistic savvy of Guirlane Duvert, with whom I discussed and reviewed all aspects of this project. Her perceptions were priceless. Joy F. Brown a great artist, and thinker, wrote wonderful introductions to chapters of this book gratuitously and organized all my work.

I am inspired by many people that I have met, but none more than Yasuko Otake a flame of inspiration. I was also inspired by Terri Davis whose sheer enthusiasm for my work helped me to escape a slow down this summer. Similarly, the encouragement of Sage Sevilla, Leander Hardaway, and Diogenes Grassal have been part of my impetus to keep on writing this book until it was finished.

Lastly, I would like to thank the great artist, James Balkovek, for his magnificent work. His artistry represents more than ninety percent of the artwork in this book. Other contributors include Rehan Mannan and vox illustrations.

List of Illustrations
(In appearance order)

List of Introductions
Written by: Joy F. Brown

The Pearls of Love

THE PEARLS OF LOVE

Poems and Stories from the Land of Nod
(a.k.a. "Trading Treasures of the Heart")

He held her tightly, to the point of breathlessness. And she freely gave up the privilege of air to be so near him. She was the sweet ambrosia of love upon his thirsty lips. He was the strong branch upon which the nest of her heart perched. They were safe. Theirs' was a true ROMANCE.

Romance

He held her tightly, to the point of breathlessness. And she freely gave up the privilege of air to be so near him. She was the sweet ambrosia of love upon his thirsty lips. He was the strong branch upon which the nest of her heart perched. They were safe. Theirs' was a true *ROMANCE*.

THE DANCE

Dance with me darling
And never leave my arms
The night wears a stunning necklace of stars
To the annual galaxy ball
She has seen how your beauty steals the show
How softly we cling together as we go
Her eyes hurl jagged javelins of jealousy
She contemplates stormy weather
Stay close to me darling
Stay close together
Let's float away this night
And safely keep from harm
While softly you press your cheek to mine
And gently grab my arm

THE PERFUMED KISS

I heard your perfume
Persuading me to be gentle
Like the kiss of dew on the lips of a rose
Then a jealous wind found us
And swept us away from the gentle night

SERENDIPITY

I met you
You stayed
We dined
We made lemonade
In a cool and scorching summer shade

THE TOUCH

Your touch healed my heart
Your kiss cured my blindness
Your love lit the lonely candle of my soul

RIDING HIGH

If you were a train
I would ride you to the last stop
If you were a plane
I'd never want to land
If you were a ship
I'd sail your heart, darling
To all that you demand

THE DIMENSIONS OF THE HEART II

The dimensions of the heart cannot be measured
The depth of a kiss is deeper than the ocean
When attached to the heart....
The height of a sigh is higher than the seven skies
When attached to the heart....
All of creation comes from love
All of creation returns to love
So tonight darling, I return to your arms
With the tender love of my immensurable heart

THE FOUR SEASONS OF LOVE

In Spring
My love was like a tropic bull
Tearing through a torrid forest of feelings
In Summer and October too
My love was like a dolphin dance
On the waves of new romance
It was astounding
And your kiss saved me from drowning
In Winter
My love was like a blue dove singing of Spring
Crowning the bull within
With dreams that were sunny and warm
And you became like mountain snow melting in my arms

THE MULTIPLICATION AND ART OF LOVE

Say, what passion can knock down the mountains?
What hand can stir the ocean like a spoon?
It is the heart that loves
The gentle embrace of a lover's face
Those satin nights of multiplied delight
Blissed by the kiss of a silent moon
It is the power of the surrender
The perfume of tenderness
The sublime tenderness of pleasing
The one to whom you owe your heart!

WHAT MAKES ME LOVE YOU?

What makes me love you?
Is it the happiness that I drink when I look into your eyes?
Is it your smile that makes the sun want to rise?
Is it the heaven in your voice that cures the blind moon and makes him wise?
Is it the glow of your being, outshining the heavenly stars as you pass me by?
Is it the footsteps of your beauty, making jealous the sea and the sky?
Is it my dreams of you and of roses multiplied by two?
When I see your lips, full of summer
None of these foolish things will move me
These things you have given all the world for free
You never made your own beauty, you see
It is a gift attached to a duty
The gift given to you for a little while
Temporary is your laugh, your luster, your smile

What makes me love you?
And from this I'll never part
It is simply and completely, darling,
The kindness of your heart

FIVE SHORT MORNING POEMS

The mind seeks to always know
Mountains seek the kiss of snow
But love prefers the pale moon's glow

I dance, mind in place
Seeking heaven in your face
Savoring a chance to embrace your waist

When we kiss like this
Heaven meets the sea
And we both become rain

The dawn sings of you
You are the moist dew of the night
Still lingering on my lips

Your beauty cures blindness
Your voice allows me to hear
That the song of my heart is still there

THE PEARLS OF LOVE

One night, without moon without stars, I was transported in space to a place beyond our Jupiter and Mars. Wherein I stood before seven humongous doors, which I believed to be the doors of paradise. I was convinced because of the exquisite perfume that enwrapped my soul, rendering me speechless and mesmerized. In addition, the seven doors or gates were resplendent embodiments of Beauty, Majesty, and Grace. One was made of solid gold.

Another covered in rare unblemished diamonds. The third was pure silver adorned with emeralds. The fourth door was awash in pearls and alabaster. The fifth was studded in rubies rare and bright. The sixth in platinum surface; and illuminated the night a sixth of the night

The seventh gate was adorned with golden pens, affixed to a turquoise ether of the mysterious question. Before this seventh door stood an angel stern and bright, carrying two swords of flaming light.

"POET!" he said, "If that is what you are, tell us, what are the two pearls of love?" "The two pearls of love are the eyes of my lady when I behold their glow beneath my face." "NAY," said the angel " you are not a poet! I tried again "They are the lips of a glass my mate gives me to sip. Lips that speak from the heart. It is certainly her kiss of love." "Nay," replied the angel "you fiddle with riddles." Then I said, " I remember when I first met her, I would have given all my time on the earth and all my heart to make her happy." "Now you have spoken the truth. The two pearls of love are time and devotion. Get down and back into the earth and find them before I will meet you a second time. Take paradise to whomever you love; and you find it there waiting when you return. Love whom you will, for you will come back alone and, perchance, you will be joined again"

With these words, the angel disappeared; and I awakened in my bed, next to the woman fate had given me. She was still sleeping; and Dawn was knocking at the door. I kissed her gently, so as not to awaken her.

I saw four rivers flowing from under my bed. One of milk, one of honey, one of wine, and the last of sparkling water. They flowed through the door of Dawn. It was time to pray and stir the day. I fixed breakfast for the both of us. She stirred, searching for me, just as I appeared with her breakfast (two eggs sunny side up). "What are these?" she asked. "These are the two pearls of love." I smiled. "Why would you cook?" she inquired. "Because I am the best cook in the house!" I said with a straight face. She laughed a happy earthquake of laugher and so did I.

I had just found two more pearls of love....

Her presence inspired him. He forgot the concept of boundaries when she was near. Therefore, he had to have her in his presence always. She was his muse, his light that flickered in darkness, his sweet song. For him longing became life's necessity. DESIRE was the sustenance that fed his need.

Desire

Her presence inspired him. He forgot the concept of boundaries when she was near. Therefore, he had to have her in his presence always. She was his muse, his light that flickered in darkness, his sweet song. For him longing became life's necessity. DESIRE was the sustenance that fed his need.

UNSPOKEN LOVE

I never knew, Darling
That you loved me
If I had known,
I certainly would have flown to your arms
Like the sparrow of the night
To a sparkling tree

CAPTURED

If you agree to be my ocean
I will ever be your river
Running to your arms
Let me in dear ocean
Its love flowing down from the mountains
I have fallen
The walls have tumbled
The castle is taken
The ramparts ripped apart and shaken
My soul is aching
My eyes, earth-quaking
Madame, you have stolen my heart!

DESIRE

I am desire
I am a fire
I always burn the ones I love

DISCOVERY

I discovered you
I swam in the deep warm waters of your kiss
The rain fell upon us like stars from a cosmic mist
Dawn descended quickly
And it was time for you to go
Night found me drifting
Walking blindly in the snow

A GLASS OF LOVE PLEASE

Pour me a glass of your love
That I may sip from its lips
And never thirst again
Then pour me another
Deeper than any other!

WHAT WOULD I GIVE?

What would I give to see you?
My eyes glimmering with hope
What would I give to hear your voice?
All the music in my soul
What would I give to hold you?
The moon and the sun, if they were mine
And the time and distance that I command
Between my heart and these two hands

"I LOVE YOU"

I words, "I love you," made the stars
The words, "I love you," made guitars
I will hold you and play the strings of heaven
And sing, "I love you,"
Till you and I
The night and the music are one

THE WAITER (Lying in Wait)

By the tree of patience
I wait for the willingness of your kiss
Then shall I claim you
Like the mighty moon claims the night

THE DIMENSIONS OF THE HEART I

The dimensions of the heart cannot be measured
The depth of a kiss is deeper than the ocean
When attached to the heart
The height of a sigh is higher than the seven skies
When attached to the heart
The touch between you and I
Is closer than the sun to its light
Closer than a bird to her song
More intimate than the morning to its dew
That is the distance between me and you
Tied to our hearts

THE BRIEF ENCOUNTER

I saw you standing there
Standing solitaire
And stylish in the morning air
I was unable to speak
So, you spoke
But I was unable to understand
Your celestial voice fell lightly upon the mattress of my mind
We touched in my dreams and my eyes bleared blind
Now, each morning I wander to and fro
Hoping to find your kiss
I beg the day to know
"Where did she go'" and "what by G-d is this?"

ONCE AGAIN

Darling, open the door of your heart
And let me walk into the Spring of you once again
Let me behold the Cherry Blossom of your soul, once again
Before the cold winds steal me from the Summer of your kiss
Let me hold you tight
Like the light of the moon holds the tender night
Hold me tight once again in early September
Before I fall into the neverland of November
And can never see you again
Love does not have an expiration date, I know
But love has a fate like the falling snow
Like the falling of time
Like the melting of poetry's rhyme
So, love me tonight, Darling
Once again…..Once again…..Once again

THE VOICE OF THE HEART

You never said that you love me
And I never said that I love you
We never wrote that anywhere
Yet I hear the music of us loud and clear
The voice of the heart is the most powerful thing in the world
It is a whisper heard above the heated din of the day
And it is a clarion bell that strikes in the silence of a Mid-Winter's night
Lighting the lamps of my footsteps toward your kiss and announcing above all things
The flutter of my heart and the arrival of Spring

I WAITED FOR YOU

A million hours I waited
I waited for you
A thousand years of tears unabated
Each day, a rose petal falls
The weeds of my heart growing tall
I know that you are the one for me
Can't you see

I waited for you
You are the one I waited for
I waited for you
You are the girl my heart was fated for
Each day that I love you
The rivers meet the sea
I waited for you
And you must have waited for me

THE SILENT FALL

I fell for you as a lonely tree falls on the forest ground
No one else was around to hear the snapping sound
Of my heartbreaking branches when I fell down
Except for G-d and the light-hearted snow who gently hugged the ground.
I was a sentinel that had to fall. I had no choice
After you passed by my gaze;
And after I heard your voice
I was simply stunned and amazed

Captured and frozen by the warmth of your grace
While all the white winds were blowing snow in my face.
Poor puzzled moon he wore a frown
As the fences of the night could not contain or confound
My dreams of you drifting down
Like snowflakes, drifting snowflakes who steal kisses from the ground
Those darn heartless snowflakes!
Those jealous snowflakes covered any footprints or clues
That might lead me to you
I'm in a bind too
I'm convinced in my mind that you are nowhere to be found
I'm just like a forlorn pine tree who has fallen in the forest of humanity.
No one saw me fall but my heart.
I am waiting silently
On the ground unable to rise
I search in the dawn each day for your eyes
Knowing someday, someway, that either you
Or the Wise Wood Cutter of Time
Will finally come around
I am lost but then shall I be found

HOLIDAYS CAN REALLY HANG YOU UP THE MOST *(a song)*

ONCE I was a proud romantic guy
Always had a new girl in my eye
Then my dream came true
I fell in love with you
We promised we'd always live in Summer
Now all of life is a bummer
Without you by my side
December's here, there's no mistaking
People online shopping, coast to coast
But I sit on the shelf, my heartstrings are breaking
Holidays really hang you up the most

School is out, and all the children know it
Angels dancing gaily in the snow
I'm a sad affair, I smile 'cause I can't show it
Holidays really hang you up the most

I remember Summer and its sweet love song
October wandered by; and leaves began to fall
Our love's a splendid thing
A thing born in Spring
Winter came early; and something went wrong

I spend time writing poems and love songs
Believing Spring will dawn her rosy toast
Can't help myself, what else could I do, Dear
Holidays are not the fun they boast

December's here, the Violets are growing
Everybody's wearing Winter coats
I sit by the fire and icy tears are flowing
Holidays really hang you up the most

Pick yourself up and keep on pushing
You make of life, the thoughts you host
Let go of shiny holidays, they always melt like snowflakes
September, November, July, February, December
Always Remember
Don't let holidays hang you up the most!!

I WAITED FOR YOU (*The song of Spring in the Winter wind*)

"Heaven always keeps astride its mystic gate, but sometimes those who love must wait. Like the Cherry Blossom waits for its sweet fruit, a persimmon seed who waits to root, a chirping, sparrow waits its turn to sing, like lonely winter waits for Spring!"

Once, on a high and windy hill, two lovers kissed in the morning mist. The sun (Mata, eye of heaven) was a witness. This happened very long ago, when spring seemed to last for a thousand years.

His name was Henry. He was tall and handsome, like Summer. She, Hikmasia was a woman of dazzling and dangerous beauty from the land of the rising sun, far across the ocean flung. She was sweet like Spring. Each day Henry and Hikmasia met on the high and windy hill; and it was Spring for a while.

Then, one day the emissaries of the Ice Emperor suddenly descended with orders to arrest and deport Hikmasia. The crime was that Hikmasia was an exquisitely beautiful woman and the jealous empress would not allow another beautiful woman to live in her kingdom. "Destroy her beauty!" the empress screamed. " Better yet, feed her to the komodo dragons on Komodo island"

So, the emissaries of the ICE Emperor (also referred to as The Orange Shadow) descended and roughly grabbed the delicate Hikmasia, as if tearing petals from a rose.

"Where are you taking her?" Henry demanded, as the emissaries slapped icy jade handcuffs on Hikmasia's gentle wrists. "Stay back Henry or we'll murder Spring and Summer, right here! We have been authorized by the 'Orange One' to deport her to 1,000 Dragons Island," scoffed the ICE emissary with the most frigid enforcement voice. "Wait for me Darling on this very hill and I will come back to you. I will come to you in the Spring. Wait and be patient please!" Hikmasia cried, with her long sad hair hanging down like a weeping willow. "It will be Spring again when I see you." An ICE emissary then covered her mouth with an ice filled cloth. "There is no return where you're going, sweetheart" the ICE emissary sneered.

"Don't worry darling," Henry replied, "I will wait for you! or I will find you « he yelled in the fecund wind, as the weather suddenly turned cold; and the leaves fell down from all of the trees who lived on the hill.

Minutes later, snow covered the entire hill where the two lovers once stood. The ICE had come and gone. They had snatched Hikmasia from Spring and threatened the promise of Summer. Yet somehow, the seasons of Spring and Summer still lived in his heart. For days and then years, Henry searched for his

Hikmasia; and every Spring day Henry came to the hill at dawn to wait for his beloved. But she was not to be found. Would she ever return? He tried every legal means to find out where the ICE had taken her. He would gladly have joined her.

Then one day he died while waiting on that hill. He died standing tall, looking outward toward the restless sea. His eyes lifted toward heaven and the horizon. He cried in his heart, "Lord, I have waited. I am of those who have faith and patience." Then he looked down upon himself. He had become a handsome persimmon tree with six ripe persimmon fruits.

For one hundred years, he stood and waited while he grew on that lonely hill with his eyes fixed upon the sea. His branches were lifted toward the sky, as if in prayer. He waited. He never hesitated in hope, faith, or patience. He hoped to one day see her again.

Then one Spring a seventh fruit appeared on his branches. It was at this time that he heard a song in the wind. It was Hikmasia's delicate voice. It was her voice in the wind. Her voice on the wing of a bright azure blue-feathered bird who had landed on his branches. "Darling," spoke the bird. "It is I, Hikmasia. Don't you recognize me? I have returned as I promised. My arms are now wings. I left as knowledge and returned as wisdom. I have returned from destiny. I love you, Henry!"

"I love you too," whispered the persimmon tree. "Never leave me again, my love." "I waited for you," she sang, "and I will never leave you again. I will build my nest and stay in your arms forever, Henry." "We waited too," shouted the hills. "We too declared the daffodils, We too shouted the skies.

Verily, time is the servant of those who love, who are faithful and endure. Love is the only pure song. Knowledge and wisdom belong to each other. Through the portrait of the seasons and the matrix of myriad civilizations, they give each other a reason to exist.

So, on that high and windy hill, they met again and again in the morning mist. Soon, by the mercy of heaven, they resumed their human form, as a man and woman once again. However, this time, they were much older.

In their old age, they became caretakers of the village orphans. Still daily, they met on the hill at dawn under that persimmon tree, who hosted their reunion.

The vicissitudes of time and fortune overtook those two. They had gone to the hill one day in May and disappeared in the mist of that morning's sweet dewy kiss. Their bodies were never found. Nevertheless, for some strange reason, the persimmon tree and a blue-winged bird who nested there, thrived for another thousand years.

During that time, thousands of lovers from the four corners of the earth and the four seasons of the time came to see the inseparable Azure bird, who lived in the inseparable persimmon tree.

EPILOGUE

The sun (Mata) was a witness to this story, as was the eye of my heart.
The moon (Bulan) was a witness to this story, as was the ear of my soul.
Heaven always keeps astride its mystic gate,
But sometimes those who love must often wait.
Like the Cherry Blossom waits for its sweet fruit
Like a persimmon seed who waits to root
Like a chirping sparrow waits its turn to sing
Like lonely Winter waits for Spring!

THE LEGEND OF THE LILY AND THE BUTTERFLY

" Stand tall against the wind and do not weep because you have lost something. Rejoice because you have everything else you need" – Dr. John S. Mannan

There once was a butterfly who was sad and forlorn. Sad and forlorn on the day he was born. There once was a Lily who lived high on the hill who had never known true love's thrill. The butterfly's name was Morgan and he was sad and forlorn because he had only one wing. Having one wing makes it difficult to fly. One needs two wings to flutter in the wind and sing in the sky, in the Spring. The two wings of a butterfly always sing when they flutter in the wind. Every creature has its song, but most men know not.

All the other butterflies laughed at Morgan because of his challenge. Some called him "The one-winged thing" or "The one-winged fling" Others teased his inability to sing in flight. They yelled cruel things like "Go back to your cocoon, Goon!" This unseemly behavior wasn't the only reason Morgan was so sad and forlorn. The main reason was that he couldn't fly south with the other monarch butterflies just before Winter; and return every Spring with his own new family of butterflies. Poor Morgan had to stay behind in the bleak northern clime.

He had to survive despite the snow, ice, and storms that would kill any butterfly any day, any hour, any time. He survived extreme weather by hanging out with his friend, the squirrel in the solace and solitude of a tree or in the Spartan den of the fluffy brown bear. The warm air from the sleeping bear's breath was just like the warmth of a cozy fireplace to a small frail butterfly. Each day and each night, Morgan prayed for a solution to his unpleasant plight. But for a very long time, there was no cure in sight.

Lady Lily dwelled in the mountain high, up in the highest hill. She lived the life of a rejected flower. There were no other flowers around her, only grass and a few brave mountain and trees. All flowers must die, we know. Some are plucked in their prime. Others are buried alive in winter snows. Others just dry up and are blown away.

All flower species have a philosophy, a belief, and a religion. They believe if you are plucked and given to someone as a gift of love, you will wake up from the dream of death as one of the flowers in the eternal Gardens of Paradise.

Alas, Lily almost made it. One day, in fact, she had been plucked from the botanical garden of the city (in full bloom). A prince presented her proudly to a commoner whom he loved, but the poor commoner woman didn't like the prince at all and toss poor Lily into a trash heap. A sympathetic wind picked Lily up and carried her to the mountain, where she was replanted alone and alive, alone and afraid; and far away from all of the other flower maidens. Lily and the Butterfly were two lonely and forlorn beings separated by cruel worlds of circumstances.

The Lily and Butterfly both prayed for better times and better outcomes. Both cried until they were numb. Both hoped that a better time would come. The wind and night are among the witnesses of heaven. So, when the wind heard these tales and wails in the night, he carried the tales of these two sad creatures to heaven on a starless night. He carried their stories to the King of Outcomes. The Lord of Destiny, he who sits alone on its throne. He created and gave light and the sun and planted the mysteries in the garden of the night. He wants the best for everyone. "I already know," said the King, "I know every leaf that falls on the floor of the forest. Go back.," said the King, "and arrange the meeting between these two creatures of mine. For my plan is must come true."

So, the wind descended from heavens (the Realm of Seven, seven skies and the seventy trillion eyes of the night) and picked up Morgan, (the one winded butterfly) and carried him to the mountains above the sea where only a few forgotten rugged butterflies dared to live. They live dejected, without a king or monarch to protect them. They lived neglected and rejected. Even their shadows despised them.

When Morgan saw Lily he fell in love immediately and suddenly his one wing began to sing in the wind. It was impossible but it happened that way, that day. That Sunday was a day of love. "What are you doing?" asked Lily, "You are a one-winged wonder!" "Singing for you." replied Morgan. "No one has ever sung for me before." smiled" Lily. "I sing Lily, because you have such beauty, dignity, and poise. Your petals seem soft and moist. And your scent is like the perfume of heaven's flowers." "You have never gone to heaven," replied Lily, "How do you know?" "With you, I am in heaven." smiled Morgan. "Heaven is wherever you are." Lily and Morgan laughed; and the two new friends danced in the wind. They danced a dance of joy that nature has rarely seen.

The grass joined, playing their blades with abandon like the bows of foolish fiddles and enchanted violins. Soon after, the nearby shrubs, bushes, and the few brave mountain trees joined in swaying to the beat of the waltz of the butterflies. The mountain rumbled in its soul. The Stars of the Night bestowed their humble light like theatrical spotlights on the stage of a brave new beautiful friendship.

The Lily loved the company of the one wing butterfly and the one-winged butterfly loved to dance with the Lily. They danced every day from Summer until the edge of Fall, when suddenly arrived a chilled nip of the air threatened to end it all. Winter and its hungry breath were near. "I don't know what to do!" grieved Morgan. "It's that lonely time of year. I don't want to leave you my Dear." "Fly South Morgan or you will surely die in these cold mountains." Lily warned. "Fly South you say?" answered Morgan, "Who me, the one-winged wonder?" "You can do it!" encouraged Lily, "You danced many days with me. Your wing is strong and powerful enough!"

Morgan gave it a try and discovered he could really fly. Not just fly, but high fly. He had muscles in his wing. He could somersault and do back wing maneuvers; and he could do all of these things with only one wing. Two winged butterflies struggled to do these things. "I will fly South," he smiled, "and I will be back to see you in the Spring, but what will you do?" Asked Morgan. "I will just hibernate and vegetate until Spring and wait for your return". Lily smiled "And then, we will dance again." "Dance we shall!" laughed Morgan as he took off Southward, riding the November never wind. Singing up a storm with his single-wing fluttering. "Good-Bye, Lily" he sang. "So long, Morgan", she replied.

Autumn begot Winter. And Winter begot Spring Soon enough it was time for Morgan to return to Lily and the mountain. Morgan returned, but he returned as a King and the father ten thousand one winged butterflies. He and his one-winged butterfly tribe were the strongest and fastest of the entire Monarch butterfly tribes in the sky. They did back flips and double dips.

The dejected and rejected exiled butterflies, who lived in the mountain, embraced and chose Morgan as their king. But Morgan was in no mood for celebration now; he was looking for his beloved Lily. He looked everywhere high and low, but Lily was not in her place. No one had seen her lovely face. He searched the mountains and valleys, everywhere, looking for his Lily. He could not even find one of her petals. Lily was nowhere to be found. "Maybe she had died or someone must have plucked her." Morgan thought. So, he searched all the houses at the foot of the mountain. Looking into their windows for Lily. Finally, he came to the window of a great yellow house (the color of a daffodil).

Through the kitchen window, on the windowsill, he saw his Lily sitting there in a blue vase of water. She was looking out of the window upon a picturesque scene. She looked both distressed and serene. A note hung on the vase which read 'Aaron loves Hypatia'.

Morgan entered the house through an open window and greeted Lily. "I am going to heaven Morgan." Lily confided, "I was given as a gift of love just before you got back. We don't have long. I have been sitting in this vase for nearly10 days." "You look as lovely as ever Lily!" Morgan said with a smile. "What will you do Morgan?" Lily continued. "I love you Lily. I want to go with you, but I'm King of the One-Winged

Monarch Butterflies; and the dejected ones have made me their king. I am responsible for the 'wing-being' of my Butterfly family." "I will wait for you in the garden of paradise, Morgan," Lily replied, "and we will dance there forever and ever." "Yes. Inshallah." smiled Morgan, as he kissed her gently on the cheek. "Bees sting. So, all flowers wait for the kiss of a butterfly who sings." Lily laughed. "Now I have lived. Goodbye, My Love" sighed Lily. "Goodbye Lily" Morgan cried and flew into the challenging turbulent skies oof the March wind. In time, the one wing butterflies became leaders of a great nation of One-Winged Monarch Butterflies

EPILOGUE

One day, when Morgan was quite old, a collector of butterflies captured Morgan in a net. He pinned Morgan to a parched cloth in a butterfly collector's book which he gave to his wife as her birthday gift. She was also a collector of rare butterflies. Morgan fell asleep in the net. "This is a rare one-winged butterfly, Dear!" Those were the last words poor Morgan could hear.

When he awakened, he found himself in a spectacularly splendid garden with rivers flowing beneath. He could hear the water gently singing on its way to the sparkling Crystal Sea. "Morgan," a voice called, "Morgan, Morgan, let's dance!" It was from Lily! "You made it, you one-winged wonder." she laughed. "I did! I did!" laughed Morgan, "Let's dance!" So, they danced, dance, and will dance forevermore, in a place where joy never tires.

So, Dear Readers, this legend of the one-winged butterfly and the Lily who lived in the mountain is a tale sung by nightingales to their children on warm Summer's nights. I am only a poor poet who regales the tales of the wind! I write of Butterflies, Lilies, and Men. All creatures who live seek love. Just remember this if you insist on finding felicity. Love and duty conquers all. When seasons of doubt wander about (whether in Spring, Summer Winter or Fall) love and duty vanquish all.

Love can turn a stone into gold;
And make a fool unfold into a king
Make a Lily's, her inner smile, behold
And crown with happiness anything
Even Morgan, that lonely butterfly with just one wing

A TIME FOR LOVE

Once upon a rhyme, there was no past, present, or future. There was no darkness or light, day or night, sun or moon, no later or soon, no near or far. There was only LOVE. No one existed beneath or above LOVE.

It was LOVE who made time. LOVE gave time a crown of twelve diadems; and a reason and rhyme to exist. This was before the sun was made and the moon kissed the face of the dark. Back then the parallel universes were only a spark in the All-Great Imagination; and LOVE infused its spirit in every aspect of creation without diminishing anything from ITSELF. Still, it is clear, that above all things, love and knowledge, freely shared, will never be diminished or impaired. Time labored alone in his kingdom of trillions of mystical clocks and watches, as he sat on the throne of a golden pendulum, which swung back and forth between the hoary cribs of stars and swatches of inner-space. Cosmic tears of sadness secretly drenched his face. Alone, he carried his solitary duties in a never-ending kingdom which continually manufactured lives and the stars.

Time had a clock for everything that was. He assigned a Clock for the time of life, a Clock for the time of death, a Clock for laughter, a Clock for disaster, a Clock for every Cherry Blossom to bloom, and a Clock in every cosmic room; and in every Bedroom, in every cosmic Kitchen, in every Mansion of the galaxies and their Black Hole tombs. Time hung a Clock everywhere and a broom to sweep away memories.

Despite all the power that he was given, Time remained sad. lonely and driven. "If only I had a wife," he thought, "then I would never be frowned upon as Time 'always lost' or Time 'rarely found'." Time was always busy running marathons between Clocks and keeping them in good repair. All those clocks and watches could never compare to one loving beating heart who loved him and really cared. So, Time asked for, and was granted, permission to marry.

He put on the robes of a bridegroom and texted an invitation to all the feminine creatures of the Universe, including the seven Mother-Earths and 'The Four' fetching female seasons. He invited all to the Main Palace of Clocks for a great pre-wedding feast!

All of the powerful female forces of nature on earth showed up including the powerfully beautiful Hurricanes, and Gales, and Stormy Weather, wearing veils bedecked with the jewels of the stars, the moon, and ten thousand perfumed nights of splendor. However, the women who attracted the wrinkled eyes of Time, most, were The Four Seasons. Time, however, as a most gracious host reserved his gaze.

SPRING was a dreamy fling of a thing flaunting resplendently the silk of her jade green frock. Her cherry blossomed hair perfuming the April air.

SUMMER showed off her enticements, as she magnificently appeared, wearing her bright mahogany smile, golden draped, brown shoulders bared. She was crowned by a shock of sun-locked hair.

AUTUMN wore her serenade of colors, exalting in her vermillion wind-tossed flair. She tangoed softly in October hearts everywhere.

WINTER, bejeweled with fine silvery hair, wore her white polar fur. Her fireplace eyes warmed the soul. Her Nefertitian neck necklaced by snow pearls, lustering in the night and cavalier.

Time could not choose, amongst these magnificently dressed seasons, which one would please him more. Their sagacity and charm could not be plainly ignored. "I'm young," purred Spring, "I have everything time needs. Everything!" "I am more beautiful, Oh King." cried Summer. "You will never want to leave the bedroom of our Universe." "Fie! Fie!" exclaimed Autumn. "You will never want to leave me. I'm wise, beautiful, generous and tall. My leaves are yours; and the ripe harvest of all my fruits!" "Oh Time," sighed Winter, "I haven't anything to give you, but true love beating strongly in my roots. I, Winter, have the greatest and deepest love of all who stand before you. I will be with you in every dream, in every room of your palace. And Darling, I will love you passionately wherever you go."

" I will marry Winter!" declared King Time. "No! No! No!" cried the other Three Seasons. "Winter is not young and has silvery hair! Do not overlook our beauty!" they whined. Time lost his temper and his patience soon declined. He, simply, could not make up his mind. "Get ye down all of you from here and come back as one duly balanced!" loudly he opined.

So, the Four Seasons united their souls and came back to the Kingdom of Time, as one united year, as a winsome, wise, and wondrous woman. "We are now One. Wouldest Thou Marry us?" beseeched the Four.

And so it came to pass, each year, when that marriage vow is renewed. And time and the seasons fall in love anew. And time and the seasons begot three children, Knowledge, Wisdom, and Understanding. Some say a fourth is now on the way; and Destiny is the fulfilment of Four. But truly only the LOVE who loves knows for sure.

Say, Oh Poet: The life of this world is like the blind shadow of time searching for an open door. The

Musicians of The Heart play the music of the key signature of Time, but only the Divine Composer knows the score.

Say, Oh Poet: Of all things on earth and in the heavens above, there will always be my Dear Reader, a time for love!

THE RUBY AND THE PEARL

There was once a ruby in the Mountain of Love that desired a pearl in the sea. She was the pearl of his soul from all eternity. It appears he knew her one time, when they were both a speck of dust. Blowing in the cosmic storms of rhyme that became the world of us. Then once, they spoke so briefly, ever so briefly, but so endearingly and tenderly. And as creation grew, they became separated. One became a Ruby in the mountain and the other a Pearl in the sea; and they never saw each other, though they had been the best of friends and the best of lovers.

Timelessness begot time, and they grew further apart, the Ruby dwelling in the mountain, that grew taller; and the Pearl in a sea that got deeper with each passing dance of the rain. But he never gave up hope. And when the winds from the ocean came to visit the caves of the mountain, the Ruby would ask, "How is the Pearl, my Beloved, the envy of the sea?' And the Wind would whisper, "She's locked in an oyster, so far away from thee." But still the Ruby clung to hope and never a word of doubting spoke (not even to himself as he lay there on that rocky shelf). The ruby's love was well known in the sea. Such was the tale of the rivers that flowed from the face of the mountains bringing down the rocks and debris, of legend built up by time and hackneyed poetry. So, the centuries passed on.

And then one day, one magic day, young boy, "Aziz" and little girl, "Aviva" whom they called "Bint" came to play near the cave where the Ruby lay. The young man was throwing the little girl's doll in the air, taunting and teasing her almost to tears. And when the doll rolled into the dim lit cave, she said, "Retrieve it now, you rascally nave." And right beside the dolly's hair, he saw the ruby lying there. "A ruby! A great ruby!" he cried; and rubbing it on his shirt with pride, he put it inside his pocket and ran straight home as fast as he could to hock it. Leaving that poor little girl standing there. Alone, in the cool sea mountain air. And that was the end of a beautiful friendship.

When the little boy, "Aziz" showed his father the great stone and how the brightness of the Ruby had shone, the old man scratched his head, awhile, and said, "Allah has given us a precious thing; for this would make a precious ring. Come, let us put it away. It'll be yours to wear one day." And time begot time, begot timeliness. Twenty years passed; and the ruby laid buried, alas, in a wooden chest beneath that house on a knolly crest.

And all the while in that darkened place, the Ruby never gave up faith. Till the day he was struck by a blinding light that broke the long and sleepless night. A voice said, "I am going to make you a wondrous thing, for tomorrow, they shall crown me King. And I shall wear you on my royal ring."

That little boy had become quite a man. In fact, the wisest warrior throughout the land. In that African kingdom of Tetuan. In the twinkling of a mystic night the time finally came, when the Ruby and the man grew great in fame. From Europe, Asia, and Samarkand came the sick, the whole, and the lame to hear the wisdom of the King and spy the Ruby's flame.

So, a year passed this way when came the feast of Shamal Nassim Bey. It was a fabulous springtime holiday celebrated on the Ides of May. It was a custom handed down by hand that gifted singers throughout the land would compete, displaying some unusual feat. That spoke in part of the prowess of their art. There was a visiting woman, from Khartoum, whose voice could make the flowers bloom. A man from Juba, whose voice could tame a lion and melt a sword of iron. But the highlight of the evening was a young woman of great beauty, who signed her name, "The believing servant of Allah, Owner of rubies and the flame."

When she sang her song all the trees bowed their heads to what sounded like the music of paradise, it's been said. And all the guests sat like ice being melted in the sun as they beheld the wondrous voice of this warm and gracious one. And her voice wove a web over their eyes. So, that sleep took some by surprise. And as she sang, it was not long before it seemed that all the birds from Tetuan had joined her song. Or so, some say who dreamed as they listened to the melody of that strange, delightful rhapsody that spoke of heaven and earth; and of G-D, Who bestows dignity and worth

The King was moved to tears; and asked, "What woman is this, that moves so near my heart without my consent? Certainly, this woman is an enchantment; some illusion of sight or an angel from heaven, sent." When her song returned its nest, he sent for her. "Woman," he asked, "Pleasure to see, who is thy father, I ask of thee?" And the woman replied, "I am Aviva, and orphan, who my father denied. I am the servant of G-D, on Him have I relied."

"Then," said the King "I will ask thy heavenly Father for thy hand; and make you Queen of half my land. Tell me, who maintains thee?" "The birds," she replied. And no sooner had she sighed, when a brilliant Blue Bird, four feet in span, dropped a pomegranate in her hand. "You see," she said, "I have no need of thee."

And the crowd gasped at her reply; for anyone who disrespected a King could surely die. This was indeed a serious thing. "Woman," said the King, "Do you know to whom you speak?" She replied, "G-D's pleasure alone, I seek. And as for thee, it's my belief that I speak with, but a common thief." For I knew you, once, when you were a boy. We were friends before you stole my toy, when you found that Ruby you turned; and carelessly our friendship was spurned. Believe me, my heart was shattered. It's just the principle that mattered."

"Ah," said the King, "I remember well the story which you tell. What would compensate for my part?" she replied, "Return the doll for a start." "This is nonsense!" the King exclaimed. I can't give you the doll! It would be impossible to find it, after all." "Well," she said, shaking her pretty head. "Neither have I my presence to give, I should never forgive you, long as I live." "And what, fair maiden," asked the King, "would substitute for the doll instead? "Only a pearl as big as your head or one perfect as your Ruby," was her reply, as fire flashed forth from her eyes. "Impossible!" he shouted, "Be gone woman, from my sight. Lest I jail you in prison, this very night!"

As she left his heart bereft. His soul was in despair (even the Ruby seemed to lose its flair). And it stayed that way. Until one day, one magic day, the King said to his vizier, "Vizier General, drag the sea; And do not fail or I'll land you in jail. Find me a pearl perfect as large as my Ruby, without defect." "By the power of Allah. In the name of Allah. Inshallah (G-D willing). It shall be done!" said the vizier, as his staff all answered as one.

Two days later, the vizier returned with a basket full of pearls, his work had earned. "My King," he said, "I report to thee, these are the best pearls in the sea." "Rubbish," said the King, "You have failed. Certainly, now you'll taste the jail." And he tossed the pearls outside. "Give these to the forbidden swine, who roam about and on refuse dine. Out! Out!" he shouted. "But my King," said the vizier, "You should come along with me, for you are an appointed King of land and sea. Perhaps the waters of the world will respond to thee and yield up the mystery."

If Allah pleases," said the King, "Tomorrow morning, I shall do this very thing." And so, in the dusk of the third morning, after he had risen to pray in that old religious way, the King set out just when the sun was dawning about. Before the sea gulls had climbed to the awning of the heavens. "Today," he said, "we shall drag the sea until she yields up her mystery."

They'd been rowing seven hours along the coastal seas, when they came to a rubied mountain that towered in the lees. The face of the mountain was the color of the King's ring. The King said to himself, "This is indeed a mysterious thing." "O Ruby," said the King, "This must be the place where I found you." And the Ruby responded by shining forth its brightest light.

The King commanded the vizier, "Lower the net. Let's see what we shall get." "Dive!" said the King, "dive!" Shouting to his five Royal divers. "And don't come back alive until you have filled the net with pearls." Very soon they tugged the line to hoister to the surface a giant oyster whose shell was red in tone; and like the brightness of the Ruby shone. When the King opened the oyster shell, he found sitting in the oyster's swell a pearl perfect of priceless price. He fell to his knees in prayer and bowed his head and hair thrice to his Lord in praise, his face toward Mount Arafat (in Mecca where the Kaaba lays)

Later he laughed like Aziz the boy. This is the Pearl," he cried, as if it was some toy. "This will turn her head." He was overcome with joy. And so, it came to pass, that the King married the little lass of his youth, Aviva Bint Solomon the wise the beautiful the pure of heart and eyes. And for her dowry he gave that girl a truly splendid thing, a gemstone from that Queen of Pearl carved into a ring. And this she wore with such great pride as she walked along by his side. And when they would kiss, they would hold hands. And the Ruby would touch the Pearl And say something like this......

*"O **Pearl**, you are lovely as ever*   *And the Pearl would sigh like the sea*
I never once wondered whether   *And say, "**Ruby** of my heart whom I adore*
You were worth ten thousand suns of waiting for."   *Please don't say any more."*

EPILOGUE

The Ruby and the Pearl are together forever
Good deeds and dreams should NEVER surrender
Love and patience soon will live in splendor, this is true for boys and girls
For young and old, for shy and bold, for rubies and for pearls
Like the Pearl, forsooth, Love is inseparable from Beauty and Truth
Like the Ruby, Love is inseparable from Truth and Beauty, Passion and Duty

For indeed the brain is the husband of the heart; and the heart is the wife of the brain
And in the Divine Kingdom of the Mind, inseparable, these Twain
These wonderous things, they live and thrive
We Poets and Pens are mere citizens of a quiet mystic place
Floating on a speck of dust in starlit outer space
Enough! Enough is said of rubies and pearls
Say the Creator is most compassionate, "The Lord of All the Worlds!!!"

THE RUBY AND THE PEARL (The Second Journey)

PROLOGUE

Through the ages and in the books of Sages, the mind and heart are inseparable. Like husband and wife, they are tied like breath and life itself. They vie for intimacy, like hearing and the ear, like beauty and the rose, like the united vision of the eyes, like the moon married to the night, I suppose.

The glimmer of the Ruby and the bashful glow of the Pearl were sublimely joined like the nearness of a kiss. Nay, even closer to each other than this, ere they in thought and scheme; and in the love and dreams they shared a thousand times ten thousand years and beyond. From the time they first met in the cosmic dust that became the world and us.

Together, they wanted to elope and abscond. Theirs was a true love bond. Inseparable! Inseparable! Inseparable (that is what they were)!

Say Poet: What false shadow dare dim such sacred tie? For love, once truly tested, will seldom die. Though the weary token of time demurely passes us by. But alas, what is good in this world is always challenged and tried. For verily, untested goodness never ever long abides. This writing is a small piece of a longer tale that I inhaled long ago and penned. A tale about a Ruby who lived in the Mountain of Love and a Pearl who lived in the Sea of Tranquility; and the way love brought them together, at last. The present, future, and past are united by time, like the transition from prose to Rhyme.

And so it came to pass, Dear Reader, that the Ruby and the Pearl were joined together for fifty years in the Land of Nod. The Ruby lived on the finger of the Great Negus of Grand Abyssinia; and the Pearl lived on the finger of his beautiful wife, Aviva, Queen of Sabab. Her singing voice could inspired flowers to bloom before their time and nightingales to chime.

It was the ninth day of the fasting month when the Great Negus passed from this world. Upon death, the King was washed, wrapped, and buried. His Ruby ring was placed in the treasure chest, since the Ruby ring could only be worn by a King and the Negus had no sons or daughters to succeed him. The entire kingdom mourned their beloved King's passing and, with equally splendid ceremony, the royal Ruby was buried in a vault, deep in the earth, until another King could be chosen. At such time, the Ruby could be seen again; and it would be Spring again. He would see and hear the voice of his beloved Pearl again. The Ruby laid buried deep in a treasure chest, deep in sorrow. He was deeply worried about his Pearl and the song of tomorrow.

The Pearl was distressed. She tried her best to put on a brave Nefertitian face. Her iridescent luster was tinged with a touch of blue sorrow which seemed to displaced any light of happiness and any hope for tomorrow. Her distress had almost stolen her mind until she called upon the divine goodness, which never sleeps and is forever kind. She entered a dream; and in the dream she saw herself with her husband sitting on a throne and five bright blue stars prostrating before them.

At which time, a crier from afar called out, "Message for Queen Aviva! Submit at once to his Majesty King Oak of the North; and he will spare your city." Two giant men, resembling oaks, carried the decree written on the parchment. These men were twenty feet tall and thick; whose bodies looked like trunks of two giant oak trees. The guards of the palace drew their green scimitars to protect the Queen. "Read your decree!" warned the Queen, "We do not permit arrogance before our presence! Read respectfully or your tongues will not be spared!!" The woodsy messengers retorted, "We are oak men and we fear not, even fire. We hear and obey our King. If you harm us, our King, the King of the North will destroy your city and everything that lives within its gates; and nothing shall ever grow here again!" "Read!" instructed the Queen, "Read!" "Oh, Queen of Sabab your honorable husband has left you and you have no protector. Marry me, the mighty King of the North and I shall give you one-fifth of my kingdom. For I am the Matchless One and wise as a serpent."

"Your Majesty, let us throw these so-called oak men down the wells of the lamp oil; and their insolent parchment with them, so that it shall become like the wicks of candle." Insisted the Queen's royal guards. 'No, no, no' said the Queen "Treat them well and give them the biggest guest room. I will answer them tomorrow. And summon to me the Ruby unearthed and superbly polished." And so, it was done.

As soon as the majestic Ruby appeared he began to smile. For he was near his beloved Pearl once again. Pearl, who was being worn on the Queen's left hand began to smile as well. Their reunion caused a bright light to emanated from the glow of their beings! "Your Majesty," cried the Ruby "I am at your service, but please enlighten me as to why I was buried and separated from my beloved Pearl!" "Oh, wise Ruby," responded the Queen, "I buried you for your own protection, so that no one would ever steal you from us! But now, Dear Ruby, I need you and your wife the Pearl to do all that you can to save our kingdom and all of our people from a greedy and wicked King who would destroy us or make us his slaves. I need to give you as a gift to the King of the North who threatens us. Perhaps you will delay his invasion and discover his weakness." The Ruby gallantly vowed, "By the power of the Wise One, the Lord of the Universes, and the Pearl of love deposited in my heart, I will give all that I have and all within my power to fight against those who seek the oppression of others. But you must promise Dear Queen to protect my Pearl while I am away from her" then the Pearl spoke.

"Dear Ruby, the lives of people are more important than ours. We existed before them; we were created that people might find delight in us, the delight of one righteous human causes the Universe to smile. What purpose has love if it cannot be offered for a higher cause? And for what good is air if it can not be breathed by a single living thing?"

The Queen then called a scribe to pen the following letter to the King of the North. "OhKing of the North, my council of Generals is prepared to make vehement war! But consider when two tigers fight and even if one wins both will be injured badly. I have powers of which you have no knowledge and I take it not for granted that you have powers too. But I ask you, Your Majesty, if by chance you win and we become your humbled subjects, is it not better to be served by subjects that love you rather than hate you? Friendship is a more reliable companion for travel in this life than warships, hardships, and weak relationships. I send you one of our most precious gems, a talking Ruby who speaks wisdom, as a token and offer of friendship."

The Ruby wept because he knew he would soon be separated from his beloved Pearl, yet again; and the Pearl wept because she knew she might never see her brave and brilliant Ruby again. "Go forth, Thou, Ruby; and sit upon the finger of the King of the North and linger there until you can stay his hands from war or harm against us!" Ordered the Queen Sabab; and it was done!

At first, the King of the North was angered by Queen Sabab's refusal to marry him. However, once he discovered that the Ruby could speak and had such great wisdom, he was mollified for a while. Soon he was smiling. By using the Ruby's wisdom to declare himself the wisest King in the world of Nod, he accorded himself visits from Kings from the North, South, East and West of Nod. These Kings came bearing treasures. They came seeking his counsel, to answer riddles, and to discover secrets and treasures hidden from eyes. Even this great honor did not satisfy the Evil Emperor of the North.

Time passed and another letter demanding marriage or war was sent to Queen Sabab. This time the Queen sent more gifts to assuage the ire of the evil ruler. However, this time she knew more about King of the North's power. Ever since her loyal subject, the Ruby, was sent to the King of the North as a spy, he and his beloved Pearl communicated telepathically in their dreams It was during these nocturnal interludes of communication she learned that the King of the North's power dwelled inside of a mystical magical oak staff call 'the serpents scepter's.

When he tapped the staff once orders were given to attack an enemy. Tapping the staff twice was a signal to retreat. Three taps of the staff cautioned his troops to wait for reinforcements. And four taps rendered instructions to destroy themselves because they would be replaced.

His scepter taps could be heard throughout the Forest Nation where he ruled. As they were repeated, a special by sound was relayed by the Soundpost Trees planted throughout the entire kingdom. Under the Evil King's jurisdiction was two armies, one he called the White Army and the other the Black Army. Each army had an Airforce of ten thousand Falcons with steel beaks and talons and an infantry of thirty thousand Oak Tree Men (each twenty feet tall and each a destructive monster). The two final armies were made of ten thousand Killer Bees each.

When Pearl was telepathed the plans of the King North's to destroy Queen Sabab's kingdom, she suggested that the Queen plant Wormwood and Geranium flowers all around the palace and the city walls (like a tightly woven carpet). She suggested a ceiling of plants be built over the city; and that the Queen sing every day which would encourage them to bloom and cover the city like a jungle canopy of green. This would protect the city because no bees or falcons would be able to penetrate the canopy (Not to mention, all bees and certain birds hate wormwood and geraniums flowers. Such flowers are well known to repel them).

After forty day and nights of preparation the Sabab kingdom was ready for war. It was able to field thirty thousand Warriors with green scimitars and fire swords, the thousand Green Falcons, and fifteen thousand Jinn. These soldiers were under the control of five Star Generals.

In the midst of all of this conflict, the Ruby was worried about his beloved Pearl. The Pearl shared the same concern for her brave Ruby. Looming was the possibility that one of them might be carried away for-ever. "Oh Queen," pleaded the Pearl "Wrap me in the three magic silken cloths of heaven (Faith, Wisdom, and Patience); and have one of your falcons drop me in the North Sea. So that I may go and rescue my Dear Ruby." The Queen hesitated crying "I cannot afford to lose you both my Pearl." Nevertheless, she granted the Pearl's request. Immediately after Pearl been dropped in the North Sea, the three magic silk wraps flew away as birds; and the Pearl was swallowed by a big fish named Nosaer.

The fish swam toward the shore and was caught in the net of a fisherman name Nebezzarazad. The fisherman was frightened when he found the huge Pearl inside the belly of the fish and ran to the King's palace to showoff what he had found. He hoped to gain a reward from the great King, by doing so. But in-stead, the Evil King rewarded the fisherman by torturing him to find out where he could find more Pearls like the one he was just gifted.

The King noticed something fascinating. Both the Ruby and Pearl would light up in each other's presence. "Are you married?" asked the King. "Yes. from the beginning of the world" they both answered. At that very moment, the three magic wraps of heaven flew into the palace window looking like birds of prey. One snatched the serpent scepter from the King's hands, the second snatched the Pearl, and the third snatched the Ruby. The King found himself helpless without his scepter; and therefore, when he yelled for the return of his scepter, he could not order and attack. Subsequently, the three birds of the magical three wraps came back to the palace of Queen Sabab with news of the capture of the King's scepter (which they carried with them).

The stunning story of the rescue of the Ruby and the Pearl, who were reunited with each other, was repeated by every town crier in the kingdom. There was happiness throughout the Land of Sabab and dwelling in the hearts of the Ruby and Pearl.

"Victory, victory, victory!" the people shouted in the streets. The King of the North was beside himself with anger. So, he commissioned a brand new scepter (more terrifying than the first) and ordered a full attack on Sabab. "Bring me the head of that insolent Queen!" He ordered. "I hate women who fight!"

The grand attack lasted seven days and nights. However, his troops (the troops of his White Army) could not penetrate the thick walls of plants and flowers that surrounded Sabab City and the kingdom. So, it left them no option, but to flee into the forest. Then the Queen tapped four times on the captured scepter and the King of the North's first Army's troops laid down their arms and surrendered to the Queen. The Evil King called up his second Army (the Black Army). So, Queen Sabab used the captured scepter again to command the first army now under her control (and without weapons) to fight the second army. The two King's Armies neutralized each other. Thus the entire war ended in defeat and humiliation for the Evil King Oak of the North.

He was captured and exiled to imprisonment in a frozen iceberg in the North Sea. As for the Ruby and the Pearl, the Queen decided to wear one on each hand, so they were always near each other (at least for a while). When the Queen clasped her hands the combined love of the Ruby and the Pearl emanated from her like a bright star. The Queen decided to put the Ruby and Pearl in charge of her Five Generals. All the armed forces, seen and unseen, bowed to the wisdom of the Ruby and the Pearl. She ordered all of her forces and their five generals to bow like bright stars before the Ruby and the Pearl. The dream was fulfilled and the Ruby and the Pearl shone most delightfully. Ah, such is the light of love one drop of love can light the heavens and earth like a candle, but one drop of hate can smash the heart like a vandal. So, Love is the conqueror and the conquest.

EPILOGUE

In time, the story of the love and wisdom of the Ruby and Pearl grew far and wide. Meanwhile, locked inside an Iceberg, the Evil King Oak of the North remained frozen and chained. Global warming came; and soon the King Oak came busting out of his Iceberg jail, loose again. Love must call to arms the power of the brain and heart. For love is an ever vexing and vigilant thing. Vexing for fools, but vigilant for kings.

She walked into the neighborhood's social club. Her presence always managed to bring class to a classless setting like this one. She sat at a table, pulled out her compact mirror with her gloved hand and fixed her lips. Every man in the room looked at her hoping for a gaze or maybe a smile. She looked at the waiter and said, "I'll take the usual." He replied, "Anything for you PASSION."

Passion

She walked into the neighborhood's social club. Her presence always managed to bring class to a classless setting like this one. She sat at a table, pulled out her compact mirror with her gloved hand and fixed her lips. Every man in the room looked at her hoping for a gaze or maybe a smile. She looked at the waiter and said, "I'll take the usual." He replied, "Anything for you PASSION."

THE LESSON

Lips thrill the night
But the darkness teaches patience
Love lights the world
To teach the heart unselfishness
Surely lovers are teachers and students of each other
Like night and day
Who chase each other into understanding\

LOVE MOUNTAIN AND THE ROSE

To break through a stone
The rose must love the sun
Though in the darkness he had begun
He heard the footsteps of her kiss
And now, darling, I give you this....
Mountains fall.
But like the rose,
Love stands tall

THE PURSUIT

You rule the dimensions of the night
I love you
I pursue you
I send you my light
How can I have you soon?
I am the sun
You are the moon

THE SEARCH

If I had searched for you among the stars
I would have found them
Making prostration to the bright brilliance of your beauty
If I had looked for you among the mountains
I would have found
That they had flattened themselves before the face of your humility
If I had looked for you amongst women
I would have found your throne
There, for none can compare
They would have hidden the treasure of your grace from my eyes
But I searched the sweet glow in your eyes
On a snowy winter night
And soon I found you there
A flame dwelling in my heart!

LOVE TEMPEST IN HEAVEN

The sun is jealous of your kiss
A morning dewdrop told me this
The moon is envious of your touch
The despondent night said as much
The stars who shine
Began to whine
When they heard me pray
For a million hours of quiet nights to love you every day!

A PRISONER OF LOVE

The first time that I heard your voice on the phone
I would've surrendered my eyesight to listen to it for a thousand years
It was a voice so poignant that it dragged tears from my eyes,
Arrested my heart
Imprisoned my soul.
I knew then that I could never escape loving you
Nor did I ever desire my freedom
Ever since I fell
I've been chained to my self-constructed cell
I live on our memories now
Eating the bread of your kisses
Drinking the ambrosia of your smile
The WARDEN gave me three wishes to choose:
Better food, Better cell, MO Better Blues
I begged him to parole me to your touch
To sentence me to hear your voice once again
To place me in the custody of your embrace.
I guess I'll die in this lonely, weather beaten place
Hoping to put a smile on your face
Thankful when, it's you, I see
Because darling I will always be
A prisoner of love!!

THE HURRICANE AND THE VOLCANO

I was a hurricane
In a hurry to discover the meaning of my existence
You were a singing volcano of passionate fire
We met turbulently on the stage of the night
Embracing impatiently beneath the stars
When dawn came smoke was in the eyes of heaven
And a cooling rain was on the way
I was burning and cold all at once
Then I realized that I had loved you, once, madly in my dreams
When I was a lonely hurricane and you a passionate volcano

THE ISLAND OF MARRIAGE

The Journey

Once I was a Prince; and I was married to five women. The first was Music, the second was turquoise Poetry, the third was History, the fourth was Law, and my fifth wife was Philosophy.

I spent splendid days and nights with each of my wives. However, I was haunted by jealousy. When I was with one of my wives, the others were always wailing outside the palace doors of my mind.

The Law was particularly demanding of my time. And Sophia (Philosophy), Oh Sophia, the enchanted sweet wisdom of her kiss made me a prisoner in her bed. I was fed up and I had lost my freedom to these wives.

I had numerous brain children by the 5; and I suspected that there was a plot afoot to assassinate my sanity, even worst, my humanity!

Then one night when I was alone, the palace nightingale entered my dreams. "Poet," he said "life is not what it seems." Then he transported my soul to the "Island of Marriage," East of my dreams and West of my imagination.

The Arrival

The Island of Marriage is a magnificent tropical island surrounded by blue waters and gifted with rivers swollen with rubies and pearls. There were two major species of trees on the island. Trees of Happiness and trees of Commitment. The trees of H0appiness had a sweet low hanging fruit; and most couples were feasting as much as they could from these sweet-smelling trees. In time, many of these lovers developed metaphysical diabetes; and were buried in unhappiness graves, wearing the three rings of their marriage. The rings were adorned with The diamond of pleasure...

The engagement ring,
the wedding ring, and
The suffering.

The tree of Commitment, on the other hand, was seven days tall and had birdcages and a large, sweet breadfruit hanging from its generous branches. The couples that ate from this tree were happy and healthy, despite the tree being difficult to climb and high up in the realms of the mind. However, the people who walked away from commitment were turned into lovebirds. Thereafter they lived in the birdcages. Looking for a way out, they pouted day and night. The successful lovers were wearing five rings adorned with the diamonds of commitment:

The engagement ring
The wedding ring
The stirring
The laboring, and
The flowering

'I am committed," I said to myself and the nightingale. "No, you are not," replied the nightingale " You must first marry the 5 wives of the self." I asked, "Who are these women within me?" "If you were a woman it would be 5 husbands of the self within you," answered the nightingale. "These spouses are your 5 human senses the sight that becomes insight and faith, the hearing that becomes wisdom and understanding, the touch that begets sensitivity and compassion, the taste that yields judgment and discernment, and the smell that embraces the perfume of intuition and unseen knowing. Embrace these. Marry these before you embrace another." Then the nightingale disappeared vanishing in the midnight air!

The Meeting

I awakened from my slumber. to find five books resting next to me. I called my five wives, but none of them answered. I was alone. I needed to find one heart to cling to, one soul to bring Spring to. But first, I would marry my heart to soul. Such a thing could make a prince a king. Then darling I will be ready for you.

THE ATTRACTION

When she first laid eyes on him, the shock and warmth of his smile lit a raging fireplace in her heart. His shoulders, broad as mighty mountains, could shelter her from the winds of uncertainty. His manner was as confident as a lion, but at the same time his eyes were gentle and caring. She didn't want him to catch her staring. So, she turned her face toward her friend, hoping that her friend might not notice her secret. "What do you think of this place?" she asked her girlfriend descending into mindless talk, while over her shoulder she stalked her prey with intermittent stealthy backward glances slightly and lightly left. He was alone. But who was he? What kind of man looked so confident, yet so strong and kind? Then she caught him staring at her. "Ah, he is mine," she thought as she flashed a warming smile, likened to ten arrows shot at once from the same bow. The arrows of her smile struck his heart, directly hitting their mark. Then, like one skilled in the art of wars of the heart, she turned her back slightly and dropped her glove lightly from her lap.

He moved in believing that he had found the cherished treasure he'd desired all night. "Madame, your glove," he cried rejoicingly, as he rushed in half kneeling. As he returned it, he gently clasped her hand. "The music and I insist that you join this dance with me." "Well Sir," she replied "If you insist and persist, I will not resist. And thank you kindly for retrieving my glove."

As they swirled across the dance floor, as if gliding on some smooth lagoon, his cologne and her perfume eloped beneath the velvet moon. "I hope that you are not going to disappear on me, like Cinderella. You have danced me into a spell, which can only be lifted by the presence of your beauty," he whispered in her ear. "I have been known to disappear, Monsieur, after first dances," she replied, clutching tightly the twin mountains of his shoulders. "What are my chances of meeting you again?" He insisted. "It depends on this next dance," she replied, as she closed her large brown eyes in front of the wings of his black bowtie. He pulled her closer, but then she gently pushed him away a little, "What is your number, Darling? He whispered." Monsieur, you must move very fast to catch gazelles and maybe sing under her window. Give me your card, that I may think about calling you." "They say it is a woman's world, Madame," the gentleman remarked, as he gave her his card. "You may be so right about that, Sir," she sighed. "How perceptive of you! She smiled as she saw the arrows still twisting in his heart. He did not know that he had fallen in the battle of love.

She returned to the seat next to her girlfriend. The gentleman kept staring at her all evening until she left. She knew she had won. His heart was in her purse. She recalled his strong mountain shoulders and kind eyes. His card gave a hint of his enterprise, but there were other cards in her purse. The choice was hers; and not his. Her arrows had conquered other men. Other voices made rivers flow within her, flowing down mountains of her imagination.

Some attractions lead to the heart's greater satisfaction. She was a master of emotional wars and all its art. She knew only a kind, honest, and unflinching king of a man could ever win her heart. Yet the night gave birth to attraction and distractions, which sometimes feel the same. So, beware of glances born at midnight dances. They may lead to love by another name.

THE CANDLE AND THE FLAME

Sweetheart,

You are my one and only flame. And I but a poor candle locked in the cupboard of the world. The mere mention of your name excites me. The touch of your lips makes me burn brightly, whenever they free me to taste your kiss. I'm in a state of bliss. I don't know how long I can live locked away like this.

You are my one and only flame; and I, a poor and naked candle. As long as you are with me, I live. I will burn hotly with the passion of you, until I have nothing else to give. It's you I must wear as a mantle Oh flame! It's you and I against the winter's windy breath, that blows too wide "the curtains of drafty death."

O flame, we were never meant to be apart. Candles and flames only share one heart. You are my one and only flame; my one and only lover. I am the candle over which you hover. Move closer, my dear, that we may discover and wear each other as garments to the celestial ball. And light the heavenly corridors of love for all.

We shall never die! Our kiss will persist as long as flames and candles exist. We will forever go and come back together again. Always, we will be the same. Same Candle; Same Flame!

In 10,000 earths! In 10,000 heavens unexplained. With persistence in every existence, your name will set the stars aflame. Our hearts are never far. Candles and flames, lights and their suns, will always be one. Our burning love is never done. Wanderers in the night. Lovers and passersby searching for the keys of life dropped from the sky will kindle us; and hold us tight. Remarking as they sigh, "Ah what a wonderful Flame you are and what a fortunate candle am I ......"

There he knelt before her, his heart exposed and vulnerable, awaiting a response to his pledge of undying love with an all-consuming look of hopefulness. She could see his plans for their future in his eyes; and this saddened her because she knew this future could never be. For UNREQUITED love yields to no one. He would now learn the lesson experienced by so many before him.

Unrequited Love

There he knelt before her, his heart exposed and vulnerable, awaiting a response to his pledge of undying love with an all-consuming look of hopefulness. She could see his plans for their future in his eyes; and this saddened her because she knew this future could never be. For UNREQUITED love yields to no one. He would now learn the lesson experienced by so many before him.

LOVE DILEMNA I (The Impossible Pursuit)

The sun cannot stay
And the moon has to go
Yet they call that an enlightened romance

UNREQUITED LOVE I

I admire you deeply
Everything you do
Everything you say
Every way about you called me to your side
Your beauty, Your dignity, Your sterling pride
The way those roses bow when you walk by
But when the sun goes down
A thousand inconsolable nights begin to sigh
Knowing sadly, you're not free and neither I

UNREQUITED LOVE II

What would I give to see you?
My eyes glimmering with hope.
What would I give to hear your voice?
All of the music in my soul.
What would I give to hold you?
The moon and the sun if they were mine.
The time and distance that I command…
Between my heart and these two hands.

THE FALLING LEAVES

The leaves fall like red teardrops
From the blue rain drenched branches of October
The Whippoorwill stops his singing spree
There is no hope in the air
The Summer in me knows that you have gone
The rain trickles down leaves into a gentle stream
Remembering that you've disappeared like an August dream
The night live streams gentle memories of you and me
Streams of what we used to be
Flowing into swollen-eyed rivers
Painful rivers who will never meet the sea

SPEAK LOVE, DEAR

The time to speak love soon disappears
Melting in hand like mountain snow each Summer's year
So much time is wasted on the chase
Night chases Dawn, never overtaking her
Grace or seeing her loving face
Then Night must try again knowing that tomorrow he will die all over again
And soon the time to speak love is gone
So even though my heart is overtaken by my feeling of love for you
What else can I do?
Speaking love into the wind is not speaking true
And now time has overtaken me too
The time to speak love disappears
Turning the pages of the fleeting years
Of a long lost and treasured musical score
Inscribed in nine golden letters
Indelibly marked, "Nevermore."
Speak love or nevermore speak
Speak love or lose forever whatever you seek!

THE SKY AND THE SEA

Once upon a time....
The sky fell in love with the sea. He heard the splashing of her exquisite voice. Day and night, night and day
under the moon and under the sun.

The sky kept trying to meet the sea, that they might be truly one.
He was sad because he believed that it could never be done.
And as the sea looked up upon his shining face,
She sang, "Oh darling I am here in my appointed place.
Prove that you love me more that I may visit you"

The Sky replied, "Madame Sea,
You are to blame not me.
Every day I see that you kiss the lips of the shore,
First at dawn and later at dusk.
You have no time for us."
The Sea sighed in reply.

"Sir Sky, you must understand.
It's not a kiss. Every morning I borrow sand.
And every evening I must return double in demand.
And that's how the beaches expand. It's in THE MASTER'S PLAN.
Besides the shore is like my brother.
And definitely not my lover"

"Oh sea who sings so close to me..."
He replied, "...will you never belong to me?"
"Oh silly Sky," she cried, "You are already my husband.

DR. JOHN (SATCHMO) MANNAN

Last night I visited your bed
And slept sweetly next to your head
Then you kicked me out

And painfully called me by another strange lover's name
You kept kissing and kissing me. And calling me Rain."
Oh, Poet, Rain is the sea visiting the Sky above
and returning home again,
Ah, such are the journeys of the heart and the vicissitudes of love
Between you and me
The sun and the sea.

SUICIDE NOTE FROM A PARKER BALL POINT PEN

Dear John,

Once upon a time, you loved me......You held no one else above me. We were so tightly wound dear when we used to write together. We wrote in the best of times and the worst of times in fine and stormy weather. We knew each other in the early dawn before the sun donned her ruby guise. You looked at me lovingly with your dreamy poet's eyes.

Then you would hold me tightly in the stormy night beneath the poet's moon. And we would write TOMES of POETRY and lively dancing tunes. You expressed yourself through me and I through you. That's how poets and their pens used to do!

I knew your touch, the touch I love so much. John, you've changed! Now the world is sad and strange; and dark and lonely.

I only have memories now. I wish I could exchange places with one of your ties. I could get by being proudly worn somehow. You used to keep me in your breast jacket pocket right next to your heart. I stayed in place in comfort and in pain I played the part (even in the rain).

I remember the time you forgot about me and sent me to the dry cleaners. I didn't complain or stain your pride, but now dear you are so much meaner.

You don't love me anymore!

There is nothing left to say. This is why you've locked me up in this dark and dreary desk drawer night and day. I never put up a stink. I never ran out of ink. So, I languish in your desk drawer -a most haunted home, deprived of liberty and light and insight

and the sacred dignity of ever writing a poem.

Baby, I just can't take it anymore!

I'm molested daily by the dark. Dying, never hearing the staccato beat of your heart. I'll never forget the day that Flossie multi-fingered keyboard walked into your life; and with a smooth-talking Mac" thing a ma jig " in tow. Little did I know that my life as a pen would be upended. My privileges as a pen suspended.

John I really depended on you!

Theirs is a culture of violence you have to hit them with fingers to make them write and type. You never had to beat me. I gave you my ink willingly and never ran out.

Then they brought a woman like talking device who is next to you day and night. She will write whatever you say with your voice.

So, Darling, I have no choice… I no longer have a voice.

"Goodbye Cruel world…"

I must go the way of the primitive stencil; and the number 2 lead pencil. Things like pens and books that people can hold have been dying old and not replaced. We've been thrown out in the deep lonely cold of cyberspace. I can no longer live in a virtual world without the virtue of love. The world is completely online. The human heart and touch have lost their cotton-picking minds.

Sorry I've lost all sense of poetry now. The old days. The good old days have gone somehow. Days of jazz and joy, when children had make-believe friends and make-believe toys.

So, John I write my final words with a hope that you will FedEx my remains to the parallel universe, where poets still love their pens and pens are not left to die alone in dark desk drawers. Where there is still balance and loyalty and love. And the greatest of these things is LOVE. Love you can touch!

So Long John!

I know for certainty there is life after Poetry; and where music goes after it is played.

Love Always,

C.C. Parker

Her front porch was the neutral zone. He was not a success or a failure there. He was just loved. She never judged his deeds. She only loved his soul. Her love was UNCONDITIONAL.

Unconditional Love

Her front porch was the neutral zone. He was not a success or a failure there. He was just loved. She never judged his deeds. She only loved his soul. Her love was UNCONDITIONAL.

I WILL BE THERE

When the sun closes his eyes and the world is dark
When rivers run away from the sea
Then run to me
I will be there

When people laugh, but you're in pain
When your favorite song is drenched in rain
I will be there

To catch your teardrops before they reach the ground
I'll be around…I'll be around

To laugh and cry and share
In Spring Summer Fall and Winter's blare
I will be the fire in the snow
The August ocean breeze we know
The song of a nest of robins in the Summer's hair
And when the maple fall
I will be there

I'll be standing tall, arms around you
Holding you close and near
Surrounding you with my love
Darling, I will be there

MOTHER: A LOVE LIKE NO OTHER

Some love is born from the fire of unrelenting passion
Some love is fashioned by tears of torrential compassion
Followed by a gentle hug that endears
Some love springs like April from the earth
Like a slow rose that takes years to grow
Some love descends like armchairs falling from the sky
Who even asks why the relationship exists?
Yet lovers young and old indeed persist
Beyond the heated golden kiss of the night
Beyond our dreams fighting for sanity and insight
There exists a greater love that dwells in humanity
A love that supports the pillars of heavens with her hands
A love that mountains over the land
Making all other loves mere mortal grains of sand
A love supreme and above any other
And that, my friends, is the love of a mother

He stood there mesmerized. Embracing her very essence. And then it happened.....she asked to dance. He breathed deeply as he gathered the courage to ask his future love's name. She looked at him, smiled with her eyes, and whispered softly in his ears, "My name is *MUSIC*."

Music

He stood there mesmerized. Embracing her very essence. And then it happened.....she asked to dance. He breathed deeply as he gathered the courage to ask his future love's name. She looked at him, smiled with her eyes, and whispered softly in his ears, "My name is MUSIC."

SAY. JAZZ AIN'T NOTHING BUT LOVE

In the pulsating poignant world of Jazz, ruby trumpets and pearly saxophones meet after dark. You will see them lustering and mustering in groups, under tall bountiful Jazz trees. They kick the Jive, their Blues, and their turquoise dreams, while sipping pints of Lush Life and Easy Living.

The horns glide trancelike closer to the stage. They know that they will soon be the rage of the night. The robust ruby trumpets recline a moment draining the last sips of warm lingering love memories, from the lips of the night before ascending to the stage.

The lush luminous curvy saxophones lag behind. They imbibe lightning tempos, while sitting on long-stem glass stools knowing that soon the souls of their feet will ask their hearts to dance to the music of the hands who play them all too well. Each musician, male and female, grabs his mate wither a trumpet or a saxophone. They will be close together for one night of forever.

Meanwhile, the bass fiddle and the drums elope their rhythms as planned beforehand. The piano is always ready to grandstand on all 88 fingers. It is consummated! The sun is asleep. The night has begun. Up goes the golden baton held above by the moon.

Ruby trumpets and pearly saxes commence that stompin' stylish tune, "Jazz Ain't Nothing, But Love."

Soon the little ones are born and running all over the place. Sharp notes and flat noted dancing at a furious pace.

We-Bop, Bebop, Show-Stopping, Jitter-Bopping, Eye-Hopping, Tip-Top, Redtop Jazz swimming in the passions of singers whose voices cause angels to dance and glance jealously at mortal romance beneath all that dancing and glancing and beyond the rose and the glove. Everybody knows, "Jazz Ain't Nothing, But Love."

What else could it be? It was composed and painted by a people who yearned to be free.

THE MEMORIES OF A MUSICIAN

I was a musician
So, when I heard her voice
Hurricane Laura started brewing in my brain
When I saw her
Then suddenly the earthquake came
I grabbed a nearby trembling breeze
"Call 911 in heaven, please!" I gasped
"I've fallen! I've fallen in love!"
Heaven came and left
The operation was successful, but the patient died
Today, I'm an old mortician trying to bury the song
Of her perfumed hair,
Hanging in the air
Playing in the wind
A memory and a tune
From the ghost of everywhere...

THE COLTRANE RIDE

I was a Jazz-head, 'CHASIN THE TRANE,' when we met on the subway train one night many, many years ago. I remember it was either on the A Train or the Blue Trane of thought. We both loved Coltrane jazz I know. Then suddenly, the music ended. When suddenly, you had to go. Then I realized that you were just a beautiful blue note, traveling to where music goes after it is played. And so was I. We are all made brief notes on the staff of life that swiftly pass by. But I do wish that you had stayed. We would have given birth to ourselves as we exited that poignant pregnant train of thought together.

Conceived as it were by our overheated imaginations, but lifetimes often pass in a brief moment's hesitation.

Years later, I met her again on the same Coltrane train that was passing through. "Well, Madame do you remember me?" with ample aplomb I said. "No. No. Monsieur " she sighed as she gently turned her head!

Then I wondered, "Can music once played be dead?" I was shocked by what she said.

I was in pain when she exited the train. And I never heard her sweet-enchanting music again. "Tickets Please!" shouted the conductor "Tickets! Tickets!"

"This is the Coltrane. The first stop is your imagination. The last stop is your imagination!

She stood there, beautifully perched, like an ancient statue waiting to be adored. And adore here, he did. She was captivating. A fellow admirer noticed his gaze and said, "She's beautiful, isn't she?" He agreed and asked her name. The fellow admirer replied, "That beauty you're beholding is ART!"

Art

She stood there, beautifully perched, like an ancient statue waiting to be adored. And adore here, he did. She was captivating. A fellow admirer noticed his gaze and said, "She's beautiful, isn't she?" He agreed and asked her name. The fellow admirer replied, "That beauty you're beholding is *ART!*"

OF POETRY AND WOMEN

Many will swear by the sun that the poetry of a woman
Lies in the sublime symmetry of her curves
Others will swear by the moon that poetry of a woman
Lies in the sweetness of her exquisite and inspirational kiss
By the stars more will say this...
Passion is a woman's singular persuasive art
No, my son! These things are far from the mark
The all-powerful poetry of a woman dwells in her heart

DISSATISFACTION LEADS TO
A CHANGE I LOVE MY DISSATISFACTION!

Dissatisfaction is a gift from G-d, a hunger pang that allows the seeds of our being to grow into a tall flowing tree, that bears the sweetest fruit. A sweet fruit that nourishes the heart and soul of ourselves and humanity.

Such beauty and wonder come from my dissatisfaction with one word that I have written; or one unpleasant note that I have played because behind that one word or note lies worlds of beauty and guarded gardens of exuberance waiting for the key within me!

The key is to discover that only perfect practice makes perfect art. And to realize that perfection/perfect art is not a destination but a never-ending symphony.

Perhaps, I am just a brief violin in the grand cosmic orchestra of existence. I'm just dissatisfied with being out of tune for one note or one word. If I address my dissatisfaction, I will beautify my one brief shining moment called "living." And beautify one small unplanted corner in the garden of life. Then I shall move on like a heart who has loved and a star who has twinkled!!

INSHALLAH. All praise due to the CREATOR

We stood there, side by side, holding hands. Love flowing from breast to breast. We cared little about what we did not have in common, that was not important. Not at this moment. We had one thing in common we loved her. And our relationships with her differed. Some of us were there because we loved being with her, some because she welcomed us in, and some because we were able to come back to her. She's our land.....She's our HOME.

Home

We stood there, side by side, holding hands. Love flowing from breast to breast. We cared little about what we did not have in common, that was not important. Not at this moment. We had one thing in common we loved her. And our relationships with her differed. Some of us were there because we loved being with her, some because she welcomed us in, and some because we were able to come back to her. She's our land.....She's our *HOME*.

THE IMMIGRANT

Children torn from breasts of love, you who cry in the night. Heaven above has indeed heard your plight. Feet pressing on, mustering at dawn against the cold north born winds. Know that Hope in battle has never been defeated; and Hope and Life are pleated journeys. The sun flush with sanguine dreams rises in your blood-shot eyes. You fly, run, swim, triathlon to portly America seeking a land of gold laid streets, abutting green meadowed dreams of freedom and opulent opportunity.

Our cities drink your faces of a thousand names. Your talents are drained and auctioned off to the lowest bidder. Yet you survive, thrive somehow, on bullet beans and rice, nanny porridge and hurled bowls of patriotic curses. You smile and never complain as you course through the vanity of our veins spacious and wide as the mighty Mississippi. You are the tired wheels of our taxis. The crusher of grapes, the wine of drunk and greedy factory machines who sing happy hour blues on industrial nights. You are the A plus student who never sleeps

You, The Mr. PC, the Programmer of JAVA scripted mornings. You serve the afternoon tea in Bel Air. You! The never late street vendor at the fair. You the wind carved on the tireless feet of human determination.

Night descends upon you like a brown moth. It finds you rummaging for the real green cards that America promised. You wonder, are they among those homeless, pregnant, discarded coke cans that litter our fruited urban plains? Or among the latest style of American dreams now manufactured in the out-source zones of our twilight's last gleaming?

LOVE PORTION # 45 (*The Manhattan Project*)

I took the long road back to myself, after my love insanity fling. First, I checked myself into Harlem Hospital's psych ward for Lovers, in THE PEOPLE'S REPUBLIC OF HARLEM.

It's a, long, sad nonprofit ride from sanity to the Psych Ward for Lovers. I caught the Metropolitan Dream Bus. I boarded the A Train of Thought Subway and rode to the last stop in my imagination. When I arrived at the Harlem Hospital Pavilion, I was directed to the "Elevatron" transporter. The Elevatron is a supersonic high-speed elevator.

It was a one half-hour trip on the rickety high-speed elevator to reach the 14th level. From there, I escalated down a supersonic escalator to the 13th level. The elevators only go from the 12th to the 14th level. Once I reached the 13th level.

I was put in irons, chained to my bed, and assigned to Room 44. To my left, in Room 43, was my old nemesis Sheik Sabir who claimed to be 600 years old and the reincarnation of William Shakespeare. He insisted he was the ghostwriter of all Shakespeare's plays. Every time I write a book he follows me, pleading his case.

To my right, in room 45 was patient # 45. A sign hung over the 6foot 4-inch door which read "Danger Do Not Feed This Patient's Ego" and "NPO". Patient # 45 kept screaming repeatedly from his room, "MAGGOTS! MAGGOTS! MEGA MAGOTS! I WON! I DID NOT LOSE! I NEVER LOSE!" From where I reclined, I saw some Mexican staff workers building four walls around room 45. The patient screamed, "Maggots! Tear down that wall!" "Don't worry senor," one of them answered, "We, Mexicans, pay for all four walls!" I was told confidentially, by a psych nurse, that patient 45 had fallen insanely in love with himself.

I stayed 45 days in this environment. They painted the walls orange and I had to look at them my entire stay. Being madly in love is okay; however, being insanely in love with self is anathema. Patient 45 was eventually moved to the honeymoon suite of the ward, where he felt more comfortable alone and isolated. Meanwhile, I'm waiting for my release papers. I'm biding my time and time is biding me.

CROCUS: THE TAO OF TWO SNOW FLOWERS

He dashed eagerly toward dawn. The war was over. He knew that his wife would be waiting. He had promised last spring that he would see her by the time the crocus flowers kissed in winter.

The crocuses appeared. Their mystic blooming petals had spoken. Stems touching tenderly, petals playing blithely and warmly in the snow, had awakened a poignant hope in his heart. He dashed. He dashed through the swirling stardust of a dream.

He was a gardener and a warrior supreme. A gardener knows the Tao of the Snow. The warrior knows that love alone conquers hearts, survives the brutal bullets of waiting and sorrow, and divines the brightest blossoms of tomorrow. He dashed. His wife sitting and waiting patiently on the porch of time, shawled in Inca blue, also knew.

Years ago, fate had planted them in a barren garden. They had grown together facing "interesting times" in war and peaceful seasons of the mind.

Winter had come, a time when petals remember their Fall; and the snow-weeds of weary hearts grow tall. She wondered if the Gardener of her heart would ever return. Would he survive? Would they bloom again? She saw a figure in the distance treading through the snow. Could this be him? Could this be the answer to her prayers? As the figure approached, her heart knew the answer. It was him, the Gardener. He had returned!

The two flowers (crocuses) that he planted next to each other a year ago had broken the crust of frozen snow. They touched tenderly as they bloomed in search of each other's arms. "Please go inside. It's cold," the Gardener insisted. "How did they connect?" demanded the Wife as she drank good news from the warm glow of his face. "Like this," responded the Gardener, enfolding his arms gently around her tender waist and drawing her lips up to his, as if deeply sipping divine ambrosia. "What did the flowers say?" The wife sighed breathlessly. "Well," he smiled; "only the husband crocus spoke, and he said that the husbands always have the last words in the house!" "Really?" remarked the Wife, pushing him away with mock rejection.

The Gardener gently reconnected and kissed her deeply, smiling inside. "Now what were those famous last words?" his Wife firmly persisted. "They were 'yes dear,'" the Gardener responded. "I thought so, my dear," smiled his wife, as the warm petals of their lips, thrived beneath late February's fickle, frigid stare; and those ice-cold wisps of winter's withering Arctic air.

The husband was home at last. He carried her inside and they enwrapped themselves beneath the warm cover of the fire. As they wore the garments of each other's hearts, the two croci bowed their heads beneath the midnight moon. "I told you he›d be back" crooned the male crocus flower. «Yes of course.› the lady flower replied, «We women do have all the power!» The male crocus just groaned amicably and sighed. It was too cold to fight and after all, they were warm and home in each other›s hearts for forever and a night.

TO VETERANS IN THE VALLEY
WHEN THE MOUNTAINS ARE NOT HIGH ENOUGH

In this world where good and evil dwell, there are a few good men and women prepared to stare down the fires of hell. They are called the veterans in this life, wherein so many claim that they care. There are those who have done much more than their share. Sir, they are our Veterans! Veterans! Veterans!

Our beloved Veterans. It's you, who carry the dreams of the people on your back, prepared to defy the ire of the fire. You lift up all of us and all of us you inspire. Even though the flames of death are calling your names. Veterans! Veterans!

You are our Veterans. Our beloved Veterans. You are the true heart of every woman and man. When others say, "We can't." You say, "We can!" You are our Veterans!

You fight for the Soul of the Nation! You push on while many others have taken a vacation from duty while claiming that they are yours truly. They spectacularly lose. It's you whom we choose! You are our Veterans! Our beloved Veterans!

It's you whom we trust. Your lives have chosen to honor us. For while others chase the green tigers of fame, fortune, and possessions, you are the few good men and women who stand against the vicious winds of oppression, hate, and aggression. You are our Veterans! Our beloved Veterans!

Oh, so many are the oceans in heaven. So many are the rivers on earth who never meet the sea. And so many are the lives who never tasted sugar in their tea. And then there you are fighting wave after wave of human apathy and bitterness. Fighting in the dark of the night and in the lonely wilderness till the dawn of hope yields the blessing of liberty and the eyes of blind hearts can finally see…..You are the Veterans! You are the Veterans!

You are the best of us. Among the rest of us. You are the brave, who gave even the extreme measure of sacrifice. You who face fire and ice; and a world of icy emotions that stare at you in bewildered wonderment, but amid all the commotions of our hearts and our emotions, you defend our freedom to live and dream of another day. You defend the notion of human distinction and dignity that way. Oh, say can we see that without you where would we be?

You are our Veterans! You are our family. Despair not. Your pains, tears, and fears knock on heaven's gate. Yours' is a wonderous fate. All of your life you will always be loved. You will never be forgotten. For you have defended all that we live for and all that we have gotten. You are the Veteran! The vision of the night. The star who often shines out of sight. We love you and always will. You defend the city on the hill; and all the dreams of human aspiration. You are hearts and hands who defend our nation and your song will be sung forever. And we will forget you never. For you are our Veterans. Our beloved Veterans! You are the sacredness of our hearts and treasure of our souls.

A BLOSSOM IS A PROMISE *(The Tale of the Mariner's Son)*

"Apple Tree! Apple Tree!
How many leaves are in your hair?
Did you count them at all my dear?
Or is it that you don't really care?
An apple please for my master!
A blossom please for my dame!
An apple stuck cudgel for the lad
Who lives down the lane
Woo, Woo Woo
Do not become unglued
Life can be easily misconstrued
So please do not be rude
If you have something to say
We will tell your story today!
"Verily, Heaven and Hell coexist in the grace and greed of men." – Dr. John S. Mannan

Once upon a time in The People's Republic of AWAKE, an old man (a retired maritime lawyer) and his son lived on a street called Blossom Covered Lane. Some say that this street is as old as time. Tucked at the bottom of a hill on West 141st, British Colonials. Rich American patriots lived there from 1664 through 1865. Before 1664, the Dutch lived there since 1656. Before the Dutch, the Lenape (Native Americans) hunted on these grounds for as long as 10,000 years. Prior to the Lenape people, Neolithic men and women slept there. And before this,

other beings lived there before the clock struck 12 noon in the living room of the universe.

That was the time when all fires burned blue and reason rhymed with desire. Space was happily married to time. Then came a new time, a new season, and a new age. When all fires burned bright red. It was an age of madness. And madness possessed the minds of men everywhere, except for a few thinkers and kind hearts. The wealthy hid from the poor and the poor hid from the wealthy, and those vicious bodyguards who accompanied the wealthy and their wealth everywhere.

The poor ate out of trash cans and dumpsters in the back of restaurants and taverns. The rich dined on caviar, steaks, truffles and other trifles of the palate. It was a two-tier society. The poor and near homelessness on Blossom Covered Lane lived underground, beneath the streets. While the rich people lived above ground in sumptuous wealth. Surely it is true that heaven and hell co-exist in the grace and greed of men.

John Henry Benton had been a black maritime sailor who worked on The Black Sea, The China Sea, The Arabian Gulf and many exotic ports of call, before he finally became a maritime lawyer. He made money from selling the cloth of his education. He spoke several languages which served him well during the trade-war recession. This recession wrought poverty to both Eastern and Western business communities. Ships were not sailing the seven seas anymore. Tariff and trade wars had led to a new level of world poverty. Only landed gentry, luxury merchants of diamonds and gold, and landlords made abundant money.

During these hard times, John Henry was constrained to doing complex translations for the court, involving a new international language called "Mandorabish". John Henry wanted his son "Joseph" (Age 15) to learn about work, how to make money and pay his own debts under the direst of circumstances. So, one Sunday morning, the two surveyed the streets together picking up bottles from trash cans. This they would later cash in at the supermarket for 5¢ per bottle. Soon they had acquired $20.00 from the bottles; and they were on their way to eat a well-deserved lunch at Soup Sandwiches R US on Adam Clayton Powell Blvd and 141st Street. While on their way to lunch, they looked up from their conversation to spy an old disheveled, seemingly homeless old woman lumbering down the street. She was adorned in a long blue dress, blue hat, and veil, and she was carrying three large bags of clothing. She seemed to be a dweller and veteran of all the seasons of homelessness. She exuded both pride and humility as she lumbered along. She also seemed slightly unhinged and troubled as she ambled along singing a strange and ancient mystic lullaby,

"Ba Ba Black Sheep have you any wool?
Yes Sir, Yes Sir
Three Bags Full
One for the Master
One for the Dame
One for the lad in blue who lives down Blossom Lane"

Suddenly the old woman stopped in front of them and greeted them humbly: "Would you help a poor old woman grab a bite, Sonny Boy?" she cackled looking directly into Joseph's eyes. "Dad can we help her?" cried Joseph. "How much do you want to give her son?" responded his father. "Half." smiled Joseph "Ten Tubmans." "Half?" Exclaimed the old woman with a hint surprise. "Oh, little lad dressed in blue always be true, we have looked for the heart that belongs to you. For 100 years, oh lad dressed in blue. Do not pursue the way of the purse. Only true acts of kindness can lift the curse of the purse." So, it was done; and Joseph handed the old woman ten Tubman's ($10) with a smile on his face "Please get something good to eat Madame!" Joseph smiled. And so, it was done.

"Now Sunny Boy, I will help you." cackled the old woman. "How can you help me?" wondered Joseph "You have nothing of your own." "Never say such a thing, young man!" the old woman scolded, as if truly annoyed. "Everybody has something unique and powerful. Now, I give you three bags of black wool; and if you take them into a bank, they will give you 13 million Tubmans. When you enter the bank, the three bags of black wool will turn into three bags of gold – woven gold. It will happen only for one who has a heart of gold, like you. This gold will pay for your education, but when you finish your education, you must serve the Ruby City and the People Republic of Harlemia with the wisdom that you are destined to receive. You must serve for 10 years, during which time you cannot leave or travel anywhere in the outside world. Can you promise that you will fulfill your promise Sunny boy? Do you believe?" inquired the elderly woman.

"Dad, should I?" asked Joseph. "It's your promise son; everyone has his own promise to keep; just like

every fruit tree has its own blossoms." "I promise dear madam." cried Joseph. "I believe." "Say it three times" the old woman counseled. "I promise, I promise, I promise!" yelled Joseph. "I believe, I believe, I believe!" "Done," cackled the old woman "you're all done." she smiled, cackled, and laughed. After which, she ambled into the Soup Sandwiches R US to grab a meal.

John Henry and Joseph sat across from the old woman as she wolfed down beef soup and a lamb sandwich. With each bite she swallowed she began to look younger and younger, until she became as young as a Junior High School girl of twelve or thirteen. "It's been a hundred years!" the young girl exclaimed in the old woman voice. Hearing the old woman's voice in a young girl's body was strange indeed. "Good-Bye Sonny Boy!" the woman exclaimed, as she walked through the glass front door, without opening it or breaking it.

As Joseph and his father stared in disbelief, the girl disappeared in three blue puffs of smoke. She just disappeared in Blossom Covered Lane's thin Autumn air. All that could be heard as she left was the sound of loud cackling and laughter in the song of the wind (a song accompanied by the strange percussive sound of galloping horses. Horses neighing and galloping, galloping and neighing, which faded suddenly into an eerie ghostly silence). She was gone. Gone with the wind. Gone through a door unseen perhaps where music goes after it's played. For indeed, where music goes after it is played is a different world filled with mystic ears. "Strange," remarked Joseph's father "Strange indeed." he repeated. "Let's follow what she said and see what happens."

Joseph and his father, John Henry, carried the three bags of blacks wool to Chase Harlem Bank; and as soon as they entered the door, the three bags of black wool became three magnificent bags of gold. And yes, it was worth 13 million dollars just like the old woman had foretold. John Henry bought a new house for him and his son. He paid for his son's education (high school and college). Joseph got a BA, MBA and Doctorate in Economics at The Universe College of Lees; and became a top advisor in the Chambers of Government He began his ten years tenure at age 25.

Joseph became a valuable advisor to the City's Fathers; and the business manager of the Ruby City, in the People Republic of Harlem. He was a wise man and people often came to him for counsel from near and far. He also became quite rich. His father, John Henry, on the other hand traveled and did business deals around the world. Tragically, he froze to death at sea when the ship ran out of power in Arctic Ocean. He was heading to Green Land. At this time, Joseph was in his seventh year of service, with only three years to go to keep his promise. He mourned his father's death for nearly a year. Then one day something unusual happened.

An old man dressed in navy blue Brook Brothers Suit came to visit Joseph with bag full of legal papers. "Your father left a lot of money for you in Vietnam, where he started a shopping bag factory. This and other investments you must go and claim, or the government will take it all." instructed the well-dressed business messenger. "I cannot go yet" replied Joseph. I have three years left on my contract with Gotham. I cannot go. Can I send you and pay you to handle these business matters? "You must go!" the old man insisted. "No." said Joseph. "I cannot go. You must bring the paperwork here, to me. I will sign or give you my Power of Attorney." "Impossible!" said the old man. "You must go in person or you will lose it all!" "I will think about it" mused, Joseph. "You have got to be crazy!" replied the old man. "I will be back tomorrow and I will make travel arrangements. You will be back in less than seven days. Only a mad man would leave such a handsome purse to be lost!" The strange old man visited Joseph every day for seven days, but Joseph still would not agree. "What's in this for you?" he asked the old man. "Five percent." he replied. "I salvage the lost fortunes of those who die. I have a private chartered plane. It seats 12 passengers. I have 11 seats filled and the last one is for you. You will be back in less than a week!" Joseph finally surrendered. "Okay, if we can return within seven days." he agreed.

So, Joseph, the old man, and eleven other passengers boarded luxury Harlem Airline King Lear Jet - Flight 777, chartered for Vietnam.

It didn't take long before the plane ran into a turbulent pocket of air. The plane shook, shivered, and rolled like a roller coaster in the Adam-Man Triangle, near the Andaman Islands. It shook with virulent vigor; as if seized and shaken by the veiled invisible hands of a wild and angry wind.

Wild are the winds of greedy passion. Wild are the winds of love and hate. And, wilder, still the wind of unknown fate. Mysteriously, the plane crashed in the green dark sea of Akaba. The dark, dark green sea of Akaba ruled by angry red winds of fate.

The angry red winds of fate are no respecter of persons. Kings have no wings strong enough to challenge them. Fools have no folly cunningly enough to fool them. All souls were lost in the bleakness of Akaba. All died except Joseph, who found himself struggling for three days and three nights to keep his head afloat. He held onto the straws of his wits to keep from drowning in despair. He was tossed, turned, and churned like a floating cube in a soup stirred by the spoon of the winds. Joseph was found by a Giant Green Dolphin who carried him out of the dangerous drink to the safety of a black sandy shore. The Red Winds abated not as Joseph lay prostrate on the beach, exhausted and spent. Soon however he was discovered by the natives of the Island. They were citizens of the Jannati, kingdom of dreams, also known as, "Dreamistan".

Men have only five senses and can perceive only five dimensions or worlds; but there are parallel worlds beyond the five, wherein live intelligent organized beings who think and love. They were a people in the Adam-Man Triangle. They were wrought from fire and invisible to ordinary eyes, the fire of imagination and intellect. Fires who burn without smoke. They were from a realm where dreams live for a thousand years, instead of one night.

The group that first found Joseph was extremely kind initially, but when they turned him over and saw his face some of them frowned. "He is an Adamite; a son of man!" shouted one of the strangers who wore a blue turban. "We must treat him kindly," cautioned another, "that is the spirit of our law and culture." "Nay," said the turbaned one, "but he has committed a crime and we owe him only justice. So, after reviving him we must take him to The Hall of Justice." Another crop of strangers came dressed in blue and red turbans. They were not kind at all. "Arrest him and bind him," they shouted, "for he has defaulted on a sacred promise – the debt of his promise! And he has failed to show gratitude for what he was given!" "The penalty, if guilty, is death," the first group retorted, "but he is injured; and our priority is Mercy." "After Mercy, we must proceed with justice." retorted the second group.

The two groups argued as to whether to take him to a hospital or to jail. Then a stranger came who wore three turbans stacked one on top of the other. "Take him to the hospital tonight," he ordered, "and after he recovers take him to the court of justice, which will determine whether he lives or dies!" So, it was done as such.

When Joseph awakened, he was shaken and grateful. Where am I?" he wondered aloud

"You are in The Empire of Dreams, a most beautiful place." a beautiful nurse answered. "This is Dreamistan the land where dreams live for a thousand years." she continued. "I want to go home." sighed Joseph "Then why did you leave?" the nurse responded, "Was it to pursue a handsome purse? Don't answer your words are recorded; and here your words will hurt you"

The next morning, Joseph was escorted to the Court of Justice. He was shocked to find that the old man who told him about his father's fortune was the main witness against him at the trial. "Guilty! Guilty! Guilty! shouted the judge loudly. "hang this oath breaker during the ninth hour of the third day." he sentenced. "Stop right there!" a voice called from the back of the courtroom. It was a man named Alton "I am his lawyer!" he said repeatedly as he approached the bench. "My client has rights, Your Honor!" "Counselor you're late!" lashed the judge. "My apologies, Your Honor. My client appeals this decision and petitions for the Mercy of the King. Justice may be late, but in a thousand battles of the heart it is undefeated!" "It's granted Counselor," barks the judge, "only if I hear the application by your client." The lawyer, in a whispered tone, provided the words that must be spoken, in Joseph's ear. "I petition the King for mercy and appeal for wise justice!" shouted Joseph. "Granted." sighed the judge. "Take him out of here!"

Joseph was dragged from the court in chains. The next day, Joseph appeared before the Great Khan, Emperor of Dreams and King of Dreamistan. "Young man," said the Emperor "you are deserving of death according to your contract and the law; but the Creator must have saved your life for a reason. Therefore, I will suspend your sentence one year, if you promise to teach ten of us all that you have learned. I will suspend it each year that I am satisfied with your efforts. Do you understand; and do you promise?" "I promise" sighed Joseph. "Say it three times young human." ordered the Emperor. "I promise, I promise, I promise!" proffered Joseph. "Good." replied the Emperor. "You are all done!"

And so, it came to pass that Joseph labored three years and three months in the Kingdom of Dreams, where he impressed everyone with his knowledge and wisdom.

Then one day the Emperor of Dreams summoned Joseph to the Royal Palace. "You have done a tremendous job Joseph" The Emperor announced. "I want to make you my vizier, my second in command. I must leave the Kingdom to put down a rebellion on Island of Drives and the Archipelagos of Emotions. The Island of Ego and the City of Conscience have joined forces; and now they all rebel against us. Will you consent to rule in my place until I return?" "I am honored," offered Joseph, "I will accept with your guidance and instructions as my guide." Whereupon the Emperor presented him with seven large keys and one very intricately made key. The eighth key was made of pure Gold; and its head was woven like expensive lace with Diamonds and Rubies intentionally sprinkled therein. "I am glad that you have accepted." He smiled here are eight keys to eight palaces. Each one has a great treasure and great power. You may open and enter the first seven, but the eighth you must never open at all. The eighth must only be opened with my expressed permission. Do you understand?" "Yes. I do." responded Joseph. The Emperor warned, "The day you open the eighth palace without my permission the Red Wind will blow, the Flowers will cry, and you will surely die!"

After securing Joseph's vow, the Emperor left; instructing all to obey Joseph. The Emperor of Dreams expeditiously departed with his twin Green Army and his Blue Army, as he set out to put down the rebels and to restore the balance of peace in Dreamistan. He left Joseph in charge of the five remaining armies (the Red, Orange, Yellow, Violet, and Indigo divisions). These divisions were on call to defend the kingdom and the eight palaces. Every day Joseph checked one of the palaces and its contents. One palace was filled with pearls from the Sea of Innocence. One housed rubies from the Mountains of Love. Another was awash with white diamonds from the Heart of the Earth. A fourth palace contained emeralds from the teardrops of dragons. Indescribably wondrous and enchanted things and amorous beings resided in each of the seven palaces. But Joseph really wanted to know why the Emperor of Dreams would give him the key to the eight palace and forbid him entry. This wonderment captured his attention; and what captures the heart's attention either frees or imprisons a man.

Joseph could no longer stand it. He was imprisoned by the very thought of what might be behind the door of the eighth palace. Simultaneously, he opened the gates of his curiosity as he opened the gate of the eighth Palace. As he opened the gate of the eighth palace, a monstrous red wind rushed out of the palace with the strength of a hurricane, while uprooting trees around the palace and smashing stones on the mountainside. It spoke to Joseph. "Lo, I am the wind of the promise that you have broken! Woe, woe, woe upon you Son of Adam for this day!"

Almost immediately after, an enchantingly beautiful young woman emerged from the palace. Joseph was mesmerized by the song of her majestic aura. It was the Emperor's daughter, "You have disobeyed my father!" she raged. "Why would you do such a thing to one who has trusted you and shown you mercy?" "Why? Why? Why?" growled the red winds of the hurricane. "Why???" insisted the princess, as Joseph gazed upon the most beautiful creature he had ever seen. At this moment, he realized she looked like the nurse who saved him in the hospital. "It's you!" he shuddered. "It's you! You are a princess?" "Yes. I volunteer at the hospital, but none know that I am Bilqueda, the Emperor's daughter." she explained. "My father is coming back. Surely, he will slay you for breaking the trust and endangering me," she warned, "because you now know that I am both a nurse at the hospital and the emperor's daughter. Until you opened the eighth palace no one, but my father and I knew this secret." "What shall I do?" asked Joseph "I am lost!"

"Tell my father when he returns that you will marry me;" offered Bilqueda, "and he may relent and be happy because he often said that he wished he could find someone like you for a son in law." "Wow!" sighed Joseph. "Of course, I will ask for your hand in marriage!"

Now the Princess was as wise as beautiful; and understood the nature of the Sons of Adam. Therefore, she said to Joseph, "Don't think that I trust you! You must sign a contract SWEARING to never leave me after we marry; and never to leave Dreamistan without my permission." "I will sign," declared Joseph, "with all my heart. I will be a servant of my word." "Then you are all done." replied the Princess.

And so, it came to pass, that Joseph and the princess Bilqueda were married; and there was happiness

throughout Dreamistan, the Empire of Dreams. The Emperor of Dreams had conquered the rebels and he happily forgave Joseph once again. Soon Joseph and his new wife Biqueda had a son named Sulayman. When Sulayman became twelve years of age, Joseph became restless to see the People Republic of Halemnia once again. He missed The People Republic of Harlem and its citizens so much. He wanted to visit his mother's and father's graves and to see some of the old friends and places.

Bilqueda saw that he was unhappy and said, "My husband, I will allow you three months to see your people and then you must return to me. Do you promise?" "Yes, My Love, I promise," said Joseph, "I know that I owe you my life!" "Then you are all done." replied the Princess "Who is the law in your world?" asked Bilqueda. "It's the Council of the Twelve Sages" Joseph replied. "They determine right from wrong. They are the wise ones who read and guide from the law that is in sky, in the earth, in ourselves, and in the books that have descended from the unseen." "It's good that you have such a law in Harlemia like the living law that we have in the Empire of Dreams, in the Land of Nod."

On the day of his departure, Joseph kissed his beautiful wife goodbye and mounted The Green Dolphin that took him to the dock of the Sky Boat. Sky Boats are shuttles that run between the Land of Nod and the Land of Awake. Daily they transverse the Ocean of Forgetfulness and sail the Skies of Oversight, where they cross the frontier of the two worlds between Wake and Nod. The third stop along the frontier of the two worlds is The Peoples Republic of Harlem (seven degrees East of the Sun and seven degrees West of the Moon).

Soon after arriving in the People Republic of Harlemia, Joseph reconnected with many of his old friends. He regained some of the properties he had once owned; and began to miss his old life of Harlemnia.

When three months passed Joseph was not ready to go back to his wife and the Empire of Dreams. When the Princess sent an emissary to escort Joseph back, Joseph refused and acted badly. Bilqueda was sad and distraught; so much so, that the second time she sent their son, Sulayman , as an emissary. When Bilqueda heard for the second time that her husband refused to come home and, and was in danger of breaking his sacred promise, she told her father, the Emperor of Dreams. Hearing this disturbing news caused the Emperor to possess the kind of anger that was akin to a fire that devours dry leaves. "I will send an army of Maziken and Genies to seize this Son of Adam in his sleep. He will pay a dear price. I will destroy the People Republic of Harlemnia for producing such a worthless Son of Adam, this Son of man!" "Don't send an army dad!" pleaded Bilqueda. "If you do, many innocent humans will die in their sleep; and the law of heaven will certainly be used against us!" "You may be right daughter," sighed the Emperor" but

I must teach these humans a lesson." "Father, I will go after my husband. I will go to the Great Council of the Twelve Sages in People Republic of Harlemia; and their leaders will bind him over to me. They have a living law like unto ourselves. I will take a squad of Genies (Jinn) and a squad of the Mazikeen for my escort. They will cross over the bridge with me between Nod and Wake." pleaded Bilqueda. The Emporer was persuaded by Bilqueda's words and said, "So be it daughter. Be careful!"

Bilqueda wasted no time. And not many days hence, she and the army her father sent to accompany her arrived in People Republic of Harlemnia; and she soon found the Court of the 12 Sages, who meet every Friday late afternoon. Bilqueda appeared before the council in her invisible form, which caused fear to enflame the hearts of the Sages. So, she hologramed her appearance to them, which was a thing of wonder as none have ever seen such a beautiful image of a woman.

"Gentlemen, you Sons of Adam, I am the princess Bilqueda, I come to you from the other side of Midnight. Our world is just as real as yours," and she proceeded to tell the whole story about her husband. The Chief of the Counsel spoke out "We know your husband quite well," remarked the Chief. "He broke his promise to us when he left years ago. We wondered what had happened to him. We did not know whether he was alive or dead. We know how to find him. We will arrest him and bring him to a hearing in chains." "Don't worry," explained Bilqueda "we can produce him before this council in the twinkling of an eye; and bound by chains that you cannot see. All we want is a trial under your law."

Immediately, the Princess and Army of Genies seized poor Joseph and flung him before the Council. Joseph shook as the Chief read the charges of abandonment. "How do you plead Joseph?" asked the judge. "Guilty, but human." Joseph replied. "It's inhuman to walk away from a promise!" warned the Judge. "Then I am guilty and do not oppose the truth." Yielded Joseph. "I will never return to the Land of Nod, or the Empire of Dreams, I refuse!" "What about your son and your wife?" questioned the judge. "What shall I do with a wife of a dream and the son of a dream?" Joseph asked. "You ventured upon this road; and now you must finish the journey. This road is not evil:" warned the judge. "I cannot!" insisted Joseph.

The trees surrounding the Court began to weep as thunder and rain fell from the sky. It was the Autumn Equinox. "What????" sighed Bilqueda? "I thought you loved us!" "I do," responded Joseph, "but we are from two different worlds." "We desire," said the Chief Judge, "that you should keep the latest promise to your wife. And we forgive your promise to us. We order that you must return and fulfill your promise to these people." "I refuse to go!" protested Joseph. "Then the penalty is death or life imprisonment." warned the Judge. "Spare him please most honorable judge!" Biqueda cried. "Yes, the penalty is death in our land too, but I do not want him anymore. So, lift the penalty please!" "Done!" said the Chief Judge. "I only request honorable judges that I be allowed to embrace my husband for the last time." "Yes of course," the judge responded, "you may." Bilqueda broken heartedly asked her deserting husband, "Will you embrace me husband before I go? This is the last time I will ever see you." Joseph extended his arms to her with tears in the eyes they hugged tightly. Bilquade would not let him go. She squeezed him tighter and tighter and tighter. Her embrace was like that of a boa constrictor's embrace. She enwrapped him so long and so hard that Joseph body became as petrified as a log of wood. Then his arms spouted other arms. These arms turned into wood and from the arms came fingers. These fingers became leaves. Soon he was a tree, an old scary apple tree.

"There you go!" Bilqueda spoke. "You will remain an apple tree Spring, Summer, Winter and Fall or until someone calls upon your name who recognizes you; and wants a favor from you. If you grant them their wish out of duty and love you will be free to decide your own fate. You will be imprisoned in the form of a tree until you keep your promise to help a downtrodden one who asks you."

With these words, Bilqued return to the Empire of Dreams weeping until she, once again, embraced her son. As for Joseph, he found himself transplanted into the forest where he was just one of many trees. He was a speechless wooden creature. He was relocated to the forest because the Council feared an enchanted tree growing within the City. Joseph discovered that there was a language common amongst all trees. A language of their very own; and every time he shared his story with the other trees they laughed at him and they cried for him. Even Josephs' worms laughed at him. He was a far cry from a man. "You should have kept your promise!" they all said. Poor Joseph just hung his head. He looked more like a weeping willow tree than an upstanding apple tree.

Then one day an old woman dress in blue carrying 3 bags of wool sat down to rest under Joseph's shade. "Sunny Boy," cried the woman, "I'm hungry will feed me with three of your best apples?" Joseph shook his leaves and down came three delicious apples unto the apron of the old woman. "Thank you, Sonny Boy. You are so generous. I've been looking for someone like you for one hundred years." As the woman ate the apples, she became younger and younger. And Joseph began to transform too until he became a handsome middle-aged man. The newly transformed woman said to Joseph, "Thanks, Sonny Boy" I now have three bags of black wool for you, if you take them to the bank they will…." "Stop right there!" cried Joseph, "I seek no riches from you, just help me get to Empire of Dreams!" "Oh well." said the old woman as she pulled a folded broom out of her hair, the size of a hairpin. She began to chant….

"Appleseed become a tree
And hairpin become a broom for me
Broom, Broom, Broom for another guest make room
Broom, Broom, Broom for another guest make room
Broom, Broom, Broom
Zoom, Zoom, Zoom away."

Up, up, up went the broom with Joseph holding onto its straw tail for dear life. The lady in blue steered it through the clouds and reach of seven worlds. Soon, very soon, Joseph was back in Dreamistan, The Empire of Dreams. His wife was still there. For dreams as beautiful as she live a thousand years. Their son, Sulayman, had become the new Emperor of Dreams. The father of the princess, the old Emperor Khan had expired when he was struck by a poisonous arrow owned by an assassin working for the King of Ego and crowned Prince OF Drives. To prevent any more revolts by the rebels against the empire, Sulayman had declared that on Mondays all people in the empire would fast during the day from dawn until sunset. This would bring the drive of the people and their strong passions and egos into the control of peace. It seemed to be working, but there were still restless citizens who didn't like to live under rules. To Joseph's delight, his wife and son welcomed him back and forgave him. Now he could restore his promise and make amends.

So this is how our story ends. A world without forgiveness is a world without love. A world without love is devoid of life. Men and dreams live side by side where Honor and words faithfully abide.

EPILOGUE

Back in the Land of Awake, Blossom Covered Lane is now called St. Nicholas Avenue. There is a funeral home named "Benton's" at the bottom of the hill, on 141st Street and St. Nicholas Avenue. It's been there for over two hundred years now. It once belonged to the Benton family, but rumor has it, that it's run by an old Romanian Gypsy woman dressed in blue. She is old one day and young the next. Her diet consists of apples (Red Delicious Apples).

I am told Dear Reader, many are the mysteries in the heavens and in the earth. They marry and give birth to other mysteries. And soon enough, all these mysteries will unfold because the mind is faster than time; and time itself is very old!

I came, I saw, I have written!!!

He ventured through time and space to satisfy the need to be. Much was lost, much more was gained. But whether by water, earth, fire, or air she was always present. She was the breadth, the depth, and the very height of being. She was LIFE. And he loved her so.

Life

He ventured through time and space to satisfy the need to be. Much was lost, much more was gained. But whether by water, earth, fire, or air she was always present. She was the breadth, the depth, and the very height of being. She was LIFE. And he loved her so.

JUST COFFEE

It was just coffee, Madame, that's all it was supposed to be
Just a sip for you; and just a sip for me
Two hours later as I drained the honey in the bottom of my third cup
A torrid revolution tempested in my cup. I knew then that something was up
That the army of my common senses could never put down
And now my little grandchildren are all running around
"Grandpa, Grandma," they say
"How do you make coffee anyway?"
"Coffee must be made with love." I said
"How do you put love in coffee?" they asked
"How could anyone do such a task?"
I replied, "Love lives in everything you share."
"If you share it love lives right there."
Now in their own homes filled with lilies and laughter
My grown-up grandchildren live happily ever after
And when I ask what gave then happiness this
They always laugh and smile and say.....
"Just coffee.....Just coffee....Just coffee with the honey of love!"
"With the honey of love in the bottom of the cup."

A DAY IN THE LIFE OF A HEART

It's Autumn!
I behold its voluptuous red and gold sprinkled smile
As I count the leaves of love, which are falling on my heart
So soon, Darling, we will have to part
And I must go wherever the winds of Destiny take me

Love me one more time
And I won't mind
When the declining Sun kisses the Sea
That will be the end of me
For I am only one day of loving you
And one day is all that I have; and all that I can be
One day of holding you
One day of embracing you
One irreplaceable kiss that drowns me in the waters of your love
Is all I need to remember; and all I will be thinking of
When Heaven rolls up the scroll of deeds
And the end of time is through
Darling, I will cherish that last sweet kiss, it's true
All that this life reserved for me
All that I was born to be
Is one simple poignant way
Wrapped in the puzzlement of a single day
One single lovely day of loving you!
I will belong to you always
So, this day of life and love is all that I shall recall
When upon me, the mystic shadows finally fall
Like bold Autumn leaves, leaving the memory of your touch
Upon the life of my heart and such
A brief shining moment as today
My love shall NEVER EVER pass away!

ONCE *(YOLO Yo-Loved)*

Once upon a time I lived
Once upon a time I loved

Once upon a time I cried
Once upon a time I died
Once upon a time
The fish of ages slipped through the net
Into the ocean of forever
And once upon a time was never seen again

THE TOWER OF RELATIONSHIPS

The building of a Love relationship between a man and a woman
Is like the building of a magnificently tall tower
Each side brings its own bricks to the worksite
The plans are written in their dreams and desires
By these two things, they are inspired
They seek to established something strong and beautiful
That will withstand hurricanes of disagreements
Tsunamis of misunderstanding and other natural relationship disasters
Sure the attack the tower
But by my eyes failing in vision
They too, will fail unless the true trust is the foundation
True patience is the frame of the superstructure
The mortar of Love is affixed between each brick
Then, the building must be sealed by the sealant of reasonable compromise
Say, Oh Poet!
"By the token of the night and its expansive heart, Love is a tower that overlooks the world and surely pride, hate, and unrelenting selfishness are the tunnels who undermine it."

THE SEVEN GARDENS OF MARRIAGE

Marriage is the right hand of G-D's government on earth
It's Bliss
It's Order
It's Wonder
It's the Majestic Seven Gardens

THE MANSIONS OF THE HEART

Oh, my love!
The Heart is a garden surrounded by myriad mansions
The dwellers of these mansions are the keepers of gardens
In one mansion lives the love of parents for their children
And the love of children for their parents
This is a mansion made of Gold
And it is surrounded by rivers swollen with Gold
In another mansion dwells the devoted love of a man for a woman
And of a woman for a man
This mansion is constructed of Rubies and Pearls, who overlooks the sea
The Rubies and Pearls sing
And call to each other incessantly night and day; day and night
In a third mansion resides those who love Justice, even if it is against themselves
Justice was married to Mercy, even before the garden was planted
The lovers of Justice and Mercy are ensconced in a mansion made of diamonds
Diamonds that sit on a mountain made of Gold
In a fourth mansion lives a kindly husband and wife, who loved Love
For the sake of gratitude for life
They shared rooms in their mansion with those who were unloved

The lovers of Love dwelled in a mansion constructed from the singing cedars of Happiness
Crowned with the dome of contentment
Supported by five pillars of wisdom high on a mountain of Gold and Diamonds
Those who do not blind
But who give insight and light to those who are kind

LOVE IS NOT FREE

Love is not given, love is not free
It has to be made each day by you and me
By the gnarled hands of patience and generous liberty
Each of two hearts has to give a part of itself
To make a third self, born from the womb of us
Love is the ultimate investment and the ultimate trust
It's win her heart or bust
It's the treasuring of life or dust
Happily ever after has to be made each day
In vigorous ovens made of life's clay
Love has never known another way
It's one plus one equals three
It's turquoise nights multiplied by two. Darling, it's you in me
And the me in you
Is the great big original spark
It's the Sun finally catching that Moon
And the loving star that they make in the dark.

ON THE RUNNING OF HEARTS AND RIVERS

Men run like cool rivers to the warm oceans of women
Carrying gifts from the mountains and hills

Like love traveling from the heart
To a thousand deeds of tenderness
Done in the thrill of the dawn
During all those memories
Of songs sung on still satin nights
Rivers run to the arms to which they belong

POEM FOR A BEAUTIFUL FRIENDSHIP

Of course, I care
Come what may
I will always be there
Until the curtain of Destiny closes on my life
And the script of me
Is torn in half
By the winds of change
I will arrange my life to always be your friend
By the token of time
By the night that hides the Pearl
By the day that shines like a Ruby
I ask the blessings of Heaven
Upon the poignant song of our graceful togetherness
Inshallah! Inshallah! Inshallah!

THE SEVEN GIFTS OF LOVE

The face of Love is indeed one of a kind
Even though the world will surely promise you its shine
Out of glass dreams, claim to have wrought a diamond shrine
I know in those quiet moments of solitude sublime

That you will always be mine
For Love is a gift to itself and its own reason for existence
Love is a river of wine from heaven
Pressed from the grapes of living and giving
My Lord has created the Sun so men could see
My eyes have been blessed to see the loveliness of thee
He made the mountains tall
I have been inspired to stand
And shelter you from all the winds
He gave a roar to the lion and the sea
And I have protected you from within
In all the seven heavens and seven earths, He hid a treasure key
The key of mind that mines all mysteries
He has blessed me to discover you hiding among the world of other women
But man is never satisfied. He is full of petitions and pleas
Wealth loses its powdered face
And from buttoned pockets flee
Yet He has blessed me to find the rich gift of companionship in your wise words
Your tender touch and such
Knowledge runs its race and falls upon its knees
At the end of life, the cupboard seems bare and cold
Nothing to take with you, but the deeds
The sacred prayers and the yearnings of your soul
But my memory of you will endure me, I'm sure
Standing our from all that I've ever known
Because of the soft, gentle, Love you've shown
Say Poet, I have climbed the mountains of our differences
I have forded the rivers of our dreams
I've fought wars over aspirations and schemes from the very start
Now it's very hard to breathe without you; and after all I may not be very smart
Because, Darling, you have everything when I gave you my heart

THE ROSE AND THE STONE

The Rose and the Stone, eternal symbols of love and fidelity, met in the gardens of a poet's mind one day. The Rose was singing ever so brightly and flirting with the sun. "Soon I will go to the gardens of paradise." she sung. "Before this very day is done." "How so?" inquired the stone, who languished in her slender shadow. "Well," replied the Rose, "when a prince plucks a Rose for his Lover (the better side of his heart), the Rose goes to Paradise. "Really?" sighed the stone. "Yes," soothed the Rose "the religion of a rose is love; and when the lover hears my song, he will pluck me and give me to his lady." "Paradise, Paradise, Paradise! I shall be planted again in Paradise!"

"What are you thinking of? "A man can't hear a Rose sing!" replied the Stone. "Not his ears, but his heart. The heart can see and hear!" Then the stone began to cry; and a small puddle pooled nearby. "I am a stone " he sighed. "People step on stones. They always throw me around or kick me when I'm lying on the ground." "Do not cry," cautioned The Rose "Crying is of no use. Crying is self-abuse. Sing, Stone, sing! Sing of love, sing of butterflies, and poinciana trees. Sing of living and giving. Sing till you smile. Mr. Stone, Sing with me awhile."

So, the Rose and the Stone sang all afternoon, 'til the moon descended in the Poet's mind and night stars closed the blinds of another day gone by. The sun rose in an azure sky and a whistling prince of a man walked by, in the garden. "Let's sing." said the Rose to the Stone. Just as soon as they sang together the prince looked down; and saw a rose and gold nugget lying on the ground. He picked them both up with a racing heart and proud hands. And gave both to the woman who owned his heart. "I'll see you in paradise." sighed the Rose. "I'll beat you there!" laughed the stone, who was now a gold nugget smiling in the sun. "The Religion of Rose is love," she cried, as she was placed in a crystal vase of sparkling water. "I love you." sighed the golden stone, as he shined from the finger of a princess on her throne.

THE CELL: A LOVE STORY

I closed my face with my hands. I would never see her bright, boisterous face again. The soft tones of her voice haunt me, even now, in this place where I will spend eternity. Still, I remain a poignant, impoverished prisoner of that engaging night of love.

We had a special connection. She was a phone number retrieved from the magic of an evening spring concert, when jazz Bossanova's rained gently upon the face of the city. Blithely in April, we rode together in a blue taxi. We touched ever so briefly as the vehicle hurdled over asphalt golf in the road. I do not know whether the touch was accidental or just destiny expressing itself. Nevertheless, the touch rocked me into believing that I would finally break out of my cell of loneliness. No voice but hers has traveled so deeply into the inner spaces of my soul. The signals of all forces involved were very strong on the night we met. We rang each other a few more times and I found out that she lived a mere three blocks from me. I liked her style immensely. I was charge up and ready to go forever.

After falling asleep one night, I awakened to find myself in an electronic trash heap of discarded items of a civilization who discards its cultural clothing every day. I saw old smart televisions, broken microwave ovens, I phones, My phones, Me too phones, Me My-selfie and I phones, and other dead but still working gadgets from an artificially intelligent matrix.

It was Tuesday. I knew this because I heard the garbage truck rumbling through the neighborhood. That would not have bothered me at all. Except, I was in the garbage truck and I was not the driver. I was in a black, smelly, and noisy abyss. I was being picked up and thrown around in circles. And while being sucked down into the dark hole of a crushing gravitational pull, suddenly I felt and heard the truck stop. I tried to call my love many times.

I then heard her singing voice somewhere in the truck next to me. "Hello," she said, "my master has discarded me. If you hear my voice, I guess we may be in the same garbage truck." "Hello darling," I responded. "I guess we are in the same truck and we've become the latest garbage of human society. This is racism!" I screamed.

Then for one brief shiny moment, I saw her beautiful black Ethiopian wrought face. "If they put me into the electronic graveyard of this fair city, then all I pray is to be next to you," I said. "Get a life John!" she replied. "We will never meet again. So, hold my body as tight as you can." I reached out to her and to my surprise, I found her in the noisy dark.

At that very moment, the garbage truck stopped and opened its giant iron jaws. We were dumped and expelled into an electronic landfill – a weeping electronic graveyard for old electronic citizens. Apple had just planted a new "I phone" in the cyber garden of Eden. Man has again eaten the attractive electronic fruit forgetting the organic kiss of touch sensitivity and love. Progress must continue as sure as the earth is round.

As for myself, I still love her wherever she may be. As long as I love her and she loves me, I believe our batteries will remain changed forever. I call her often but maybe she cannot answer me just yet. If you see her or hear her distinctive ringtone, please text her my Samsung MET Id so we can talk tower to tower. Tower to power. Tower to flower 1-1259-6614-3511-1918. Tell human beings not to call me. I am dead and they live. At least that's what they think.

Someday we will visit our oppressors who buried us alive while we were still working and in the prime of our lives. Human beings wouldn't treat each other so shabbily. Would they? Could they?

Sincerely yours,

"The Cell!"

THE ALLEGORY OF THE CAGE

"By the token of time, men begin as brothers of the Cage. Only a few escape the rage of ignorance, but most languish behind its invidious invisible bars."

Once upon a time in the land of Nod, The Blue Scholar and his wife, The Green Scholar, lived in a large apartment building overlooking the Hill of Tranquility. The apartment was seven stories high. Beneath it was a valley of cities and cyber cities. The two thinkers were very much in love, but not more than the two love birds who were their pets.

The two love birds (also husband and wife) lived in a large golden cage in the living room. The door of the cage was always open; which allowed them to flitter, flutter and fly freely throughout the entire House of Light. The only enemy that the two lovebirds shared was a red house cat who was always looking to catch them by surprise and to make a quick meal of them.

The Red Cat was named "Tim." Tim was always watching the mystic clock that hung on the living room wall. He acted as a pet, but he competed against the lovebirds for his masters' attention.

One fine day during the ides of November, the Green Scholar had been baking bread and honey. The Blue Scholar opened the living room window to cool off the extremely warm apartment. Seeing an opportunity to obtain freedom, the male love bird bolted for the open window and flew into the shivering winter sky. "Free at last! Free at last! Great clouds of thunder, free at Last!" chirped the newly liberated lovebird.

The Blue Scholar, upon witnessing the escape of the love bird, became very upset and excited. "Ungrateful bird!" he shouted. "You will freeze to death or be devoured by a hawk, owl or falcon! Did you not enjoy our hospitality? We fed you, protected you, educated you. We loved you!"

The Green Scholar was also upset. She was a singer and enjoyed the male love bird's grand male voice. The Green Scholar cried uncontrollably as she tried to regain her balance, "Why did he leave us?" she wondered.

Then the female love bird spoke to her masters. "Master Blue, Scholar of the sky and Master Green, Scholar of the Earth, my husband did not understand the dangers of the unknown. We just wanted to be free." "Why didn't you go with your husband?" sighed The Blue Scholar. "Were you afraid to leave with your husband?" "No Master Blue" replied the lovebird. "But why would I substitute a bigger cage for my small cage? You humans live in cages too. It's a big cage of your own making. You live in invisible cages of your own limited vision. Bars of fear, Bars of ignorance, Bars of hatred, and Bars of greed keep you grounded like worms. You humans can't fly. Instead, you live like worms. You cling to earthly possessions, waiting to be devoured by your own feelings."

"I am a free thinker!" shouted the Green Scholar. "So am I!" protested the Blue Scholar. "You will see," warned the love bird, "that you live in a cage just as I do. You have enslaved me; and we are all enslaved by the bars of time. With the exception of those who are free in mind. The bars of greed and the bars of fear are all there. You are blind to bars of the mind that cages a man in his own thinking!"

"I am a free man!" cried the Blue Scholar. "Not some savage bird who lives in a cage" he added. "I will prove it!" said the Blue Scholar.

So, the Blue Scholar descended by the mystic elevator seven stories, until he reached the first floor of the lobby of the void. For the first time, he felt as if the building was hanging over the cliffs, as if being held by a string. The building swayed back forth in the wild and wise winter wind. He looked out at the gray sky with great fear. Bars were growing up everywhere like a magic field of bamboo stalks all around the building. It was clear that they all were living in a giant bamboo cage. This cage was hanging and swinging on a most slender string.

There were 4 gates or entrances in the lobby of the void (North, South, East, and West). To the North was a courtyard and gate. The Blue Scholar exited the gate and looked up at the building swayed back and forth like a pendulum in the sky, like a bell ringing on high. Suddenly a huge vulture called "The Vulture of the Culture" entered the yard and began eating everything in sight. He snapped down bushels of words that were flying, through the air, like fireflies. Soon the North Gate had many bars. They were living in a cage!

Next, the Blue Scholar entered the South gate. Outside the gate, he saw bins full of treasures guarded by green tigers. People were trying to chase away the green tigers. However, each time someone tried to pick up a handful of diamonds or rubies, the Green Tigers devoured the mind of that person. Soon the bars of greed covered the entire gate area.

Next, the Blue Scholar went to the East Gate. There he met three women (Mary, Merry and Marry). Each was so beautiful that the Blue Scholar forgot for a minute about his wife, whom he had left alone, crying. As he stared at the beautiful women; and was unable to unfix his gaze, new bars grew up around him. These bars blocked his exit to freedom. These bars are called "lust". Inside them, many men were lost, stolen or strayed in the rage of the cage.

Lastly, The Blue Scholar opened the West gate. Outside that gate was a maze of tunnels and electronic games. These tunnels and games tried to swallow him by sucking him down into a large black box, like a giant vicious vacuum. Downward it pulled with the irresistible appetite of a galactic swirling black hole. The Blue Scholar resisted the maelstrom with the power of his meditative mind. "Lord," cried the Blue Scholar," I lived forty years on this earth and I never knew that I lived in an invisible cage!"

"A cage that confines and defines me!"

"A cage that blinds me and is not kind to me!»

Soon an old beggar entered into the cage and into the building from outside. "If you feed me," the old man offered the Blue Scholar "I may show you a way out. But must you go back and free all the other people in your building. If I show the way the out, you must do this. The love birds will teach you words of the heart, but I will show you the ways of knowing." "I will save only myself and my wife!" cried the Blue Scholar. "I'm not responsible for others. I do not love others. I am a man of wisdom." The Blue Scholar continued to answer in the negative; and could not find his way home to guidance. The beggar sat and waited.

The love bird who had been looking out of the window succumbed to The RED CAT, who surreptitiously swallowed her. Her time was up! The window was still opened; and the male love bird hastily returned. But it was too late to warn, pick up or save his wife. Tim the cat had already swallowed her.

With his wife gone, the male love bird closed his cage. No no other bird could enter therein. He then turned toward the window and flew out into the wise and wily winter wind. Love needs freedom and freedom needs love.

The Green Scholar paced and paced. Finally, she sat there in the middle of her mind. Love needs unselfishness to allow it to breathe. And unselfishness needs love to express itself. All else is the rage of living life in a cage.

She cried and wondered if her love, The Blue Scholar, would ever return to her arms (or would he be forever lost in the rage of the cage).

The old beggar sat and waited in his place. The Red Cat also sat, staring at the Green Scholar with hungry mystic eyes. They would wait. They would all wait. So too the invidious Cage waits, who captures the minds and hearts of men. Only love and guidance can save them. The love of freedom, the love of wisdom, and the love of wanting for others the things that you want for yourself. Then comes the guidance who unlocks cages seen and unseen.

THE MIGHTY WALL WHO FELL IN LOVE

"There are seven walls in the mountains of the mind
And seven gates to heaven divine
Search the time and turn to the right
You will find no wider gate or taller rampart
Then the mystic gate who speaks in the night
Or the stony wall which covers the heart"

Introduction

The night has seven gates that guard the paths between the fortresses of the day and the castles of the night. Once upon a time, the seventh gate spoke to me in the night. She was the keeper of my dreams. She invited me inside to discover a sad and joyful mystery buried deep beneath the veil's history. This is a story about a relationship between a girl and a wall. A tall tale you say. How can a stone or a wall have a relationship anyway? All things have a purpose therefore all things have their self - lives and shelf lives.

All things are usually committed to the purpose for which they were made. Whether it be the sun, the moon, or their shade. What we wrongly call "things" are alive. Some "things " even have husbands and some, "things," wives. Is not the sun married to its light? Does not the day court the night, giving its light to the moon like the rose of a kiss? Yes, there are many examples like this. They're in our oceans in our

skies, and in ourselves. In the sadness and the bliss of moments of our lives, things designed to serve us like mother nature may even revolt against us.

Even our shadows, one day, might revolt when they disagree with the mad directions of our lives. But that is another story!

After things serve their purpose they crumble or fall. Whether a tumbleweed or a mountain tall, or a silver star falling from the sky. Except that is when it happens that a thing falls in love. When someone or something falls in love, it inherits a power beyond the reach of time. Love is a power who conquers the realms of all minds. Seen and Unseen. When in love, a thing once a servant becomes a king or a queen! Soon enough you shall see what I mean!

The Story

The year was 1863. It was on the Ides of April. The gates of war between the North and South of the United States had long fallen off its hinges; and the dogs of battle were ripping out each other's throats. On the cotton plantation of Mr. Ponchatrain, in Randolph Virginia, the owner had erected a huge 30-foot wall made of 400 stones called the Ponchatrain Wall. This wall was designed to keep black slaves from running away to the freedom they longed for. The wall was deemed particularly cruel because "Massa Ponchatrain," as he was called, put poisonous spikes on the wall. These spikes caused the victims of an escape attempt a very painful punishment, which often resulted in death.

On April 15, 1863, Massa Ponchatrain was packed and getting ready to join Robert E Lee's Confederate Army. He would leave his wife, "Cruel Mary," in charge of his 144 slaves. These slaves were forced to worked from dawn till dusk in the fields during the day-and work in Massa Ponchatrain's whiskey still at night. "Cruel Mary" was given her name because she devised creative ways to torture and punish slaves for the slightest infraction.

The day that Massa Ponchatrain left is the same day that IFAS arrived at the Ponchatrain plantation. Ifas was 15 years old and was given to Massa Ponchatrain by another cotton planter to settle an old gambling debt. IFAS was a most beautiful and graceful girl Her mother was from the Ashanti people and her father, Woodruff Culpepper, a cotton planter.

That first day Ifas arrived, she was tied over a log and given 15 lashes to "teach her Godly humility," according to Cruel Mary. Ifas was then placed in the cotton fields with the others; but was given the odd morning task of cleaning and trimming the walkway, in front of the Ponchatrain wall. This walkway was awash with flowers growing on both sides. It was during this time that Ifas and that solitudenous wall first met each other. As Ifas adapted to plantation life, she was regularly beaten by Cruel Mary and locked beneath kitchen chambers of 'The Big House,' as Massa's mansion was known. One morning Ifas was so badly beaten on the soles of her feet (bastinadoed) and she could hardly walk. She made it to the wall and tied her feet with a wet cloth to soothe the wounds.

Cruel Mary, who was rotund and wretched in appearance, was very jealous of Ifas's beauty. This is why Ifas's punishment was so severe. Ifas wept profusely as she leaned on the wall, her face buried in the bend of her arm. "I am alone, my Lord!" she cried " Send me a sign of freedom!" Her wet tears soaked into the stone; and a remnant of them trickled gently onto the grass. She often cried and prayed at the same spot; and her tears were absorbed by the same stone. In time (at least a year), a blade of grass and a gentle violet flower grew from that tear-soaked stone in the wall. When Ifas saw the bright beauty of the flower growing on such a stone-faced wall, she said aloud to herself and the flower, "Oh flower, how could such a wondrous flower grow on such an evil wall. A wall that killed the dreams of my People?" The wall coughed and IFAS ran away in terror as if from a bad dream. The next day she returned, she saw two flowers growing from the stone. "What kind of wall is this?" she whispered under her breath.

"You dare malign my character!" gruffed the wall, " You are lucky I'm not a swallowing wall! My ancestors, in the enchanted East, used to swallow the enemies who touched them!" Ifas was in utter shock. «I'm not afraid of you!» she replied, mustering her soul and heart to aid her wavering voice. "You shouldn't be!" corrected the wall. I didn't design myself, I am a slave to whomever designed me; but I have a good heart." "Maybe you do," Ifas replied, "after all, those two beautiful flowers grew out of you."

"These flowers, that grew out me, are watered by your tears," the wall demurred, "never curse the mud if it produces flowers. These flowers prove that there is good in both of us." "Wow!" sighed Ifas, "A talking wall!" "My Ancestors go back to Babylon, to the Hanging Gardens of Nebacanezzar and the wall that spoke to his son Belshazzar. I have a cousin in China (The Great Wall of China) and another in Africa (The Great Wall of Zimbabwe). And you, daughter, are the thrice great-granddaughter of the Mansa, King of Mali -an Ashanti man who journeyed to this land long ago by sailing the moon and the twinkle of the Sirius Star."

The Wall began to tell Ifas about her great history. He enlightened her from dawn until the noon sun stirred from his bed, for the second shift of the four mystical watches of the day. "How do you know so much?" asked Ifas. "We walls are one family in the world. We know when one of us has fallen. The wind delivers the news. I have a subscription to the clouds. "Go, Ifas Go! They are looking for you!" insisted the Wall suddenly, "You are in big trouble!" When Cruel Mary saw Ifas, she had Ifas bound to the wall; and ordered Mansour, the strongest male slave on the plantation, whip her 13 times. When Mansour protested, Cruel Mary had Mansour whipped thirteen times as well. It would be two weeks before Ifas found herself in the company of the Wall again, but this time she went to the wall with Mansour. The wall spoke to both of them, swearing them to secrecy.

By this time, twelve flowers had grown out of the face of the wall. Ifas and Mansour talked about escaping together to the other side of the mountain, beyond the wall. «Push hard on the center of my heart, where the flowers are blossoming. There dwells my heart and the softest part of my soul." instructed the wall. Crawl through me to freedom and follow the river to its mouth. There, you will meet a man named Green. He will guide you to safety, where you can wait until the war is over. Once you've arrived, wait there until the night you see face of the Wolf Moon sipping from the drinking gourd of the stars and opening the mysteries of heaven. It will look like this...." The wall revealed a stellar drawing on his face. It was a rare configuration of stars. "Why are you doing this for us?" asked Ifas. "Because I love you, Ifas," replied the Wall, "ever since you placed your tears on my heart. If I were a man, I would challenge Mansour to a duel for your love." laughed the Wall. "But alas, I am a wall and not a man.

Now, Mansour you must promise you will take good care of her." "I will," promised Mansour, "with all my heart." "One more thing," added the Wall, "when justice is done, return after the war and tear me down so that I will not harm humans with the poisonous spikes placed within me.

You will find a treasure hidden in me, buried by a runaway slave named Moses. When you tear me down, the treasure will belong to you and your people as the beginning of reparations and I will be free at last! "

About a year later in late 1864, The Wolf Moon drew very close to the Big Dipper in the drinking gourd as if it was drinking from it. Ifas and Mansour together pushed through the heart of the wall and crawled to freedom. They travelled along the river, for 40 days and 40 nights, until they reached its mouth and met a giant of man dressed in green. Even his skin was green.

"I am Mr. Green; and I've been waiting for you two." he said. "Let's catch some fish!" So, they caught and ate fish until they were satisfied. Mansour and Ifas fell asleep after eating. When they awakened the Green One was gone. In his place was a fishing rod, made of gold. For a while, Ifas and Mansour fished in the waters of their faith, Down By Riverside, alone from dawn to dusk and dusk to dawn. They received the news that the war was over and returned to the Ponchatrain Plantation.

Massa Pontrachain died at the Batlle of Gettysburg and Cuel Mary was whipped and hung by a dozen of her slaves (May G-d forgive all thirteen souls). With the help of the freed slaves, Mansour and Ifas tore down the Ponchatrain Wall. The Wall went quietly into the dawn of its afterlife and in the memories of men. "I love you Ifas!" were the last words that The Wall spoke.

Epilogue

The treasure of a sack of Ponchatrain gold was divided among the freed slaves equally. Ifas married Mansour and they lived happily ever after. Well almost! It does rain sometimes. Once upon a time, a gate spoke to me in the night. Spoke to me of love. Spoke to me once, of a mighty wall who fell in love!

THE RIDDLE OF THE RIVER AND THE "A" TRAIN OF THOUGHT

"There is a river between life and death; and every man must cross the water of his deeds. There is a river between happiness and regret, between greed or desire and what we really need. Ponder the straight path of the river; and do not run adrift in the weeds along the river of life."

Introduction

I have known love and love has known me
The love between a man and woman I have known
The love between a father and his children I have known
The love of a child for his parents, I have known
The love between a man and his community I have known
I have pursued wisdom, art, and mythology as if they were women
All these loves kneel before the throne of the GREAT LOVE between a man and his Creator
All these rivers of existence flow into and from One Love
So, I write this poem as I return to the great ocean of humanity from which I came
I have known love and love has known me
Rivers are destined and designed to meet the sea!

The Journey

Whether one is rich or poor. Whether one owns a palace or not even a door, service is indeed the only throne that elevates the heart. I have lived in a tent by the river of the contemplation of eternity for a, very, long time. I am ready to move whenever the river floods again. My tent will become a sail; and I will sail to the seas of tranquility. I am ready Lord! I am ready!! I have solved the riddle of the river!

My Predecessor State

My predecessor (my old self) lived here before me. He was not ready when the river came. His palace did not float, nor did it become a boat. This was the riddle of me, myself, and I. My predecessor, my present self and my future self are finally united. So, my fate is the fate of all men who ponder. O, my people! My orphaned fatherless people. A people without memory are fatherless. So, faith and hope have become our foster parents in a foreign land. It was we who gave birth to love and optimism "Down by the Riverside". We gave birth to our new selves, our new identity (for a while). Sometimes I feel like singing. Sometimes I wonder why I should be not winging like a bluebird across the Summer sky. The kiss of the sun is gentle. The eyes of my daughters are beautiful. The arm of my son is strong. The embrace of life has many poignant moments. Sometimes I enjoy the luxury of living in one of them. When I do find time to think, it's like giving a diamond to a stranger (even if that stranger is myself).

The River

By the waters of the Harlem River, I sat and I wept, as my soul remembered the Jordans of Africa. An Africa far away and far removed from my American identity. Africa is my distant past, my distant father. Jamaica was my recent past, my recent father. There in the land of my recent father, the mangoes dem walk tall. And the breadfruit dem talk all the time, to old wise men sitting and eating saltfish and ackee by the sea. I was not there when my great-granduncle, Marcus Garvey, came to New York. I was not there when a million revolutionaries danced on his tongue before launching revolts against mental plantations and gray matter colonization affecting my people. I, John, was born in the storm! But the storm was normalcy for me. You ask me many questions and I respond, "How can I ever throw my pen into the river? My pen is my sword! My sword is my mind! And my word is what I write. And so I exist!

This recovered from my first intrinsic struggle with identity. Identity is Ground Zero. My first identity is human this morning, as I look in the mirror. There will be no mourning. I look in the mirror as a child of the river of life. My face is Black, like the skin of the sun. Like the pit of a Black olive. Like the Black sandy beaches of St. Kitt's Dominica or Punaluu. Like the Black pearls in the luminescent sea. But this is not really me! It is only a sign leading to other signs. My Blackness is a garment, the silken thread woven by The Fashioner, a mere garment woven in the loom of history. Humanity focuses on the garment forgetting that man is mind!!! For, very soon the garment is torn asunder and we leave it behind, to be worn by descendants or next of kin in the genetic line. Life is as brief as a grand peal of thunder. Life is a drop of rhyme in the ocean of wonder. Only our deeds and prayers survive. They are the ferry boat we ride and the Captain, who crosses with me to the rivers of the other side.

You see, there are traffic lights on all these rivers that flow through the streets of Harlem. They have nothing to do with traffic. They don't control traffic. They control progress. When you see things that make you pause or doubt the goodness of humanity -for example, a mugging, a street fight, a fallen addict-the light turns red. I used to stop and stare like the rest of the crowd. However, when you see something that makes you smile, even a "good morning" greeting the light stays green. We've got to keep Harlem green and prosperous for all people. Especially for both the people who are being pushed out and pushed in by society's invisible hand. Rivers can come together and become a mighty chorus when each River has found its own voice. I am John, the son of John the Conqueror born in Harlem. My first battle is to navigate the river of myself and then to join the others.

My Vision of The River

Have I seen rivers, you ask? Yes, my son, I've seen rivers! Black rivers and white rivers. Rivers of day, rivers of night, rivers of sorrow, and rivers of joy, Sun rivers, moon rivers, rivers that won't meet tomorrow. Troubled rivers that worry and annoy. Rivers that flow beneath gardens of mangoes and passion fruits. Rivers, swollen with trees of pain that have blood on their roots. I've seen rivers so many rivers, rivers in my life and time. I've seen rivers of class and rivers with pedigree. Rivers of poverty, rivers of gold, rivers young and rivers old. Rivers of ice, rivers of fire, rivers of sadness, passion and desire. I have seen rivers longer than those of the original Langston Hughes poem; longer than one of John Coltrane's jazz solo saxophone. Yes, my daughters, I've seen rivers! I've seen rivers of glee. Rivers that retire, rivers of unwanted sympathy, rivers blind with desire. And muddy like the Colorado River of tears that flow from my eyes. Rivers of fears that I despise. Rivers of sorrows; Rivers like no tomorrows!

I've seen rivers!! Rivers of gladness, I've seen. Rivers of sadness and unrequited love. Yes I've seen too many rivers. Rivers that will never meet the sea. Rivers that flow from you to me. A river that flow from me to my destiny. Rivers! Rivers! Rivers that are lost, Rivers of pride, Rivers that I am afraid to cross, lest I find myself on the other side. The East River, The Hudson River, The Harlem River. I've seen all of these except the mighty River of Jordan; and I'll see that one too, in the Bye and Bye…..Bye and Bye…..Bye and Bye…..

Gentrification

I Remember the hordes! The gentrification's soldiers who came from the South, the East, and West of Ivory Gotham, from Tribeca, Yorkville, Chelsea, from Eastern Long Island and New Jersey. Huddled like that tribe of Attila the Hun, they crossed the rivers of the city and emerged from the dark woods of Central and Riverside Parks. Yes, indeed, terrifying hordes like the moods of Macbeth or jealous ivory Othello. Block by block, they stormed the brownstones. They evicted the Brown renters who had dwelt here in Harlem for over one hundred years. Arresting them with rent increases and crucifying them, Spartacus-style, with eviction notices up and down the Aplan way of 7th Ave. (Adam Clayton Powell Blvd). But these renters were poor urban Sharecroppers on the mental plantation. Orphans in businesses, they had not banded together to buy Harlem or taken over its abandoned stores since the time of the great migration of the 1920's and 1930's. Do not weep for the gentrification of Harlem. Weep for the ignorance of those who beg with tin cups while sitting on stools of gold. Renters disunited are urban sharecroppers on a mental plantation owned by the Emperor of 'A Dollar and a Dream'.

Leaving Adolescence

I decided one day, before I was 25, to leave my adolescent frame of mind. This happened when I saw the refugees of gentrification leaving Harlem to cross the River of the Bronx. Soon with the same thinking, they will be evicted from the Bronx. What is next, Canada? Eventually, Black Harlemites may find a warm place for rent on the North Pole. A place from which one can never be evicted except by Polar Bear landlords. Oh, how many more rivers must we cross, I wondered, before we learn to stand up and buy our freedom. Not one by one, but together! I decided to leave my adolescent train of thinking. After I get ff my ferry job, I will take the A Train uptown just to ride the tracks of my memory one last time. It was Harlem, after all, that made the A train rhyme! The "A" train and I were both born in Harlem. Today may be my last day operating the ferry on the Harlem River. I want to find warmer waters in my olden and golden years. The Republic of Harlem is 3/5 under water, like the Italian Venice of old. But I heard that the A train is still running and I can catch it going south. It now runs under the Atlantic Ocean all the way to Africa. That's why it is still called the "A" train. But the Africans are still coming here. I guess life is a two-way street!

This time when I ride the "A" train, it will be for a higher purpose than just transportation. For most people going to and from work and school, the "A" train is just a tin covered, rented, coffin shuttling souls between morning cups of coffee and moribund states of mind. I need to find that Duke Ellington/ Billy Strayhorn "TAKE THE A TRAIN" of thought, that stops at different stations of inspiration. I understand that the real "A" train is painted a Bebop shade of Blues and runs "ROUND MIDNIGHT." It is time to face reality. Harlem will change forever. Forever, means until the next gentrification cycle or hiccup in the economy. I have finally crossed the river of accepting change. It usually involves lessons that cause us to ditch the dirty diapers of closed mindedness and wear the adult underpinnings of self-help; and the full spectrum of human possibilities for excellence and exuberance, dignity and distinction.

The Arrival

I sat by the waters of the rivers of Harlem. Waters flowed down my cheeks. Water flowed, too, over the Banks of the sidewalks. Water caused the gutters to come alive. There were lives in the gutter, hearts in the gutter. Side-walkers and stoop-sitters were in the gutter. There was a man in a wheelchair trying to cross to the other side. I took him on my back and swam with him until I reached the shores of 116th Street and Malcolm X Blvd. There I heard Church bells ringing. I heard the Muslims' call to prayer from the dome of Masjid Malcolm Shabazz/ Malcolm Shabazz Mosque. Hearing the Church bells and the Muslim call to prayer mingled together around noon was an astonishing experience! Men of all faiths were warming themselves around a large black metal barrel that was filled with burning charcoal and wood. It was cold, but we all warmed ourselves around our common Humanity. We wondered what we had in common and how we differed. Then we discovered our human identity; and the rivers subsided and drained back into the drainpipes and sewers that ran to the sea. The People Republic of Harlem, for one brief shining moment, became beautiful like a garden surrounding the jewel of a city. A city in the heights! A city on the hill! All life flows down to the sea of eternity; and up to the sea of the real reality!!

What is the riddle of the river? River, River, River, where do you run?

You were once many; now you are just one! My lunch time is over. It's Winter in Harlem again. It's raining a cold Blue rain and I've come to a stoplight again. I'm waiting. The light is still Red; the raindrops are still Blue and river of the streets are still Black as the asphalt night. The light is still Red but I've decided to keep forging ahead. I am not going to let the Red lights of life stop me.

Ferryman is my job. It pays well in my retirement and we eat fish every day. Yes sir! River whiting and porgies caught right in the Harlem River. There's an old man in me. There's a young man in me. They have frequent nuclear wars against each other (M.A.D.). Sometimes the old man and young man see eye to eye. Most times, they just fight and smile. I don't know what ferry boat can join us together. I just know Jordan River is chilly and cold. And soon, my soul must take its own ferry to meet me myself and I on the other side. My sweet Motherland will be waiting in that Great Gettin' Up Mornin'! My Ma will be waiting. My Pa will be waiting. My Love will be waiting. Waiting and singing, near the mouths of Rivers of Honey, Milk, Sweet Water and Wine.

Epilogue

I, John, am your brother and partner in jubilation and tribulation. I was born in the Republic of Harlem. I live and I die in the Republic of Harlem EACH DAY. My son and I own the Ferry boat now. I always keep the keys of freedom, like a lifeguard, around my neck so I can free any man who is searching for the truth route to freedom. I am also always watching the tide, for the Hour awaits me (and I await the Hour) when that old man and I will stand before my Lord. For too many years I had lived in a tent next to the river of eternity. I sometimes fished in the waters of my weakness. Its fare was pleasant to the taste, but bitter in my stomach. I fished in the waters of philosophy, near Hell's-gate, where the East River meets the Harlem River. I had many a sumptuous supper, but those fish are somewhat extinct now. So, I became emaciated and lost too much weight. I fished in the waters of love for the sake of a love that I could call my own and for while I was fat with happiness. My net was always full. I gave many fish to my neighbors in the desert. One day I returned to the fish trap I had set. But the fish (the dessert) had escaped to the sea. I fished in the waters of my strength; and it provided all I needed for me and my family for a while. Time then fished my strength from the waters of me. Ah, such are the rivers of a man! Rivers of achievement are real but some rivers who plan never meet the sea. These rivers run aground in me. And I in them!

I found a river that runs straight through paradise. Composed of the waters of collective work and informed faith. It connects the hearts of men to the rivers of paradise. Freedom lies in the heart and the intellect, giving service to all creatures for the love sake of The Creator of all Creatures. This is only the river of peace and empowerment that reaches the sea of satisfaction. One last thing, the "A" Train really does run from Harlem to Africa three times a week! Yes Sir, Friday, Saturday and Sunday! Once you reached Canal Street, the "A" train goes under the Atlantic Ocean. The next stop is Dakar Senegal. The engineer is Duke Ellington, the Minor Third, and the conductor is Billy Strayhorn, The Major Fourth. Don't worry, it's a glass-bottomed train with submarine features. Once you have reached Africa you will see a very old African woman (319 years old) walking up and down the beach crying and holding an ancient Black baby do ll. The doll reminds her of her child Kwame, snatched from her arms in 1562 by the crew of Captain John Hawkins leasee of the good ship 'Jesus'. If you see her, tell her Kwame made it. She will stop crying for a while. She refuses to die until she believes that her son has been saved. Every time they put her in the ground, she comes back and walks on that beach again. Sing this song to her and she shall become a 20 years old mother again, nourishing Kwame inside the cradle of her womb.

"Harlem river is chilly and cold
We have crossed the Jordans of old
Rivers are one community
Like you and me
All flowing to the sea
Building sacred strength and Unity"

There are millions of people that carry my Ancestor's name, the Kwames. I sit by Harlem River and wonder which one was my ancestor. Kwame is my thrice great-grand uncle. Verily, he is waiting for me on the other side of HISTORY…on the other side of THE RIVER. There is no doubt, I am an ancestor now. May those after me remember me, and if not me then my works. Scribe, I am leaving two boats in my will. They are moored on the Harlem River. One is for a new body of knowledge to be transported back to the community life. KNOWLEDGE THAT TRANSFORMS INDIVIDUALS A ND COMMUNITY!!! The second boat is for the travel of the spirit, the travels of the souls of my people to safe and sound optimistic destiny. Destiny is determined by decisions; and decisions are made by a strong-headed ruling royal couple in these parts. Medically and metaphysically called the brain and the heart. Maybe I will name my next son "Kwame".

"Rivers are riddles who find answers in the sea."

He stood at the crossroads, perplexed and frustrated. Then she appeared. She walked softly, but he felt every step as she approached me. She held a pomegranate in one hand and an ostrich feather in the other. She kissed his frowning brow, whispered great words in his ears, and opened his eye. As she walked away, he asked her name. She replied, "I have many names, but you may call me WISDOM."

Wisdom

He stood at the crossroads, perplexed and frustrated. Then she appeared. She walked softly, but he felt every step as she approached him. She held a pomegranate in one hand and an ostrich feather in the other. She kissed his frowning brow, whispered great words in his ears, and opened his eye. As she walked away, he asked her name. She replied, "I have many names, but you may call me WISDOM."

ON THE RELATIONSHIP BETWEEN MIND AND HEART

Who will separate a pearl from its luster?
Who will separate the sun from its shine?
Who will separate the heart from her husband?
The inseparable mind!

ON THE RELATIONSHIP BETWEEN WEALTH AND LOVE

If a rich man traded his riches for love
He would be called a fool
If he traded love for riches
He would be called a scoundrel
But if a man never loved, he never lived
To become a fool or a scoundrel......

ADVICE TO A SON I

If you love a flower, water it gently and keep it far away from the storm
If you love a woman, shower her with kindness and consideration
Keep her secure and far away from uncertainty

ADVICE TO A SON II

If you are free, solvent, and you love a legally available woman of good character
    who is inclined toward you
Run to her, claim her, and cherish her
Lest regret become your wedding ring and uncertainty your bride

ADVICE TO A SON-IN-LAW

Love is work
Love is forgiveness
Love is compromise and compassion
It is more than looking magically into someone's eyes and saying, "I LOVE YOU."
It's saying I want the best for you
Love is trying to multiply happiness by two...
After it has been divided by two
It's the new math and old math of heaven and earth
A lightning rod married to lightning
A mystic baton conducting a concert of reconciliation
Between storms of ice and storms of fire

THE WIFE OF LIFE

Wisdom is a late bloomer........
I never saw such a flower in Spring. When I was young, I believed that Life belonged to me. I believed that Life was my wife; and I could seduce pleasure from her by living her. As I grew older, I realized I belonged to Life; and I was one of the billions of husbands serving her. Life taught me to serve all living things with love. I argued with Life sometimes, but we never went to bed angry. I finally realized that I belonged to her as much as I thought she belonged to me. I realized that when I cross the River one day, she will take another husband. I will look back across the River and realize how much I love and miss her. I will see her smiling in the wind, holding to her lips the wisdom flower that I gave her on the day that I gave birth to myself; and made her my bride. Ah, such is my love......Such is my life!
Such is the pride and joy of living.......LIFE

THE COSMOLOGY OF LOVE

Planted seeds of knowledge
In the heavens, in the earth, and in ourselves
By knowledge, the mind of man is enriched and satisfied
When knowledge is shared it bears more fruit
And the garden of knowledge soon becomes as bright orchards of stars growing and glowing
Until they illuminate the heavens and the earth
The water of thirst makes a seed expand
Filling and refilling the fertile mind of a man
Nevertheless, love preceded the light
Love was the very first kiss of night
She placed a portion of herself in a pitcher on the nightstand
In the sacred hall wherever brightness and compassion were gathered, together
Every time a man drank a glass from the pitcher of love it refilled itself
Every time he shared a glass with another the pitcher expanded and water became more satisfying
The giving of love satisfies the heart
The receiving of love brings happiness to a soul
Love and Knowledge
These two gentle things turn mountains into gold and fools into kings!
I John, bear witness by the night and by the lips who whisper the sacred secrets of her light.

OF LOVE, BEGGARS, AND WISDOM

There was a man, who had no legs, begging in the subway. He said, "Woe is me. I lost my legs in the war." I gave him a coin; and he smiled.

There was a man in a wheelchair trying to cross the street, but the curb was too high. So, I helped him up the curb; and he smiled.

There was a blind man selling pencils, standing on the corners of Hope and Change. I dropped a coin in his hand, but he cursed me! "Why do you not love me? Why do you dishonor me?" he asked.

"You were born with eyes, but you are blind. I was born blind, but I see. Please do not deprive me of work's dignity. It is better that you give me NOTHING."

I left, I slunk away. I did not smile all day, but I learned wisdom from that insightful blind man. Sometimes giving is taking. Sometimes taking is giving! Sometimes love is showing respect and not compassion. Sometimes love is the simple passion to maintain and sustain dignity in all we see.

THE MANGO AND THE CACTUS

There was once a mango tree who was blessed to give birth to the sweetest, juiciest, most perfect fruit for a thousand Summers. Her arms stretched from the sea to the river; and all men, animals, and bees sought her shade and succulent fruit. She bragged loudly to all the other trees (the durian, papaya, avocado, carambola, guava trees) and the lowly cactus. All in earshot of the wind, that flowed through her leaves, heard her swagger song. "Never shall Winter touch me, for my fruit is the most favored in the land. And indeed, I am worthy to be honored among all trees in the garden."

The other trees complained and bemoaned that their fruit was not as sweet. All complained except the lowly cactus, who was thankful for his spines. At last, Winter did come; and Winter was followed by a withering drought which dragged on through the Spring, Summer, and Fall. At last, the Mango tree shriveled to the size of a bush and died. All the trees shriveled, shrunk, and died. All except the lowly cactus, who flourished in the desert and gave birth to a flower. And that flower is Gratitude. And Gratitude is love.

FRUITFUL PROVERBS FROM MY PEN

"If you have love within, share it. If you find love around you, harvest it. Then share it."

"Love is not free, but it frees the heart. And what frees the heart? It is the rope of consistent commitment."

"A fool will love many times, but all wise men know that they are fools."

"Knock on the door of love while the door is still there. For someday the door of its opportunity will surely disappear. Then you will weep. For what you never had, you could never keep."

"Light the candle of love and avoid all the windy drafts of severe emotions."

"I have climbed the red mountain of love. I have climbed the blue mountain of reason. I have found that love must have reason."

"Speak love now or forever search for peace."

"I went to the dance of life without a partner and came home with a partner. I went to the dance with a partner and came home with a broken heart. So, too when I approached life with preconceived ideas, I was disappointed when I did not find truth and beauty anywhere."

"I came, I lived, I loved. My heart was reborn. These are the four seasons of me."

"Fires in fireplaces are servants of the home. Fires not contained are masters where they roam. Passion without love is like a fire without a place. Fires without a place become harsh slave masters, burning lives around them with fiery disaster."

"Look not for a day that will bless the heart. Rather, it is the heart who must bless the day."

"A tear not shed floods the soul. A smile withheld detonates the heart."

"Better to conquer a heart than vanish a city. For one who conquers hearts shall find the city at his feet."

"Wind without a destination dies. A heart without love does not live, it simply weeps between each beat."

"The beauty of Merit is better than the merit of Beauty......

But joined together, these are the modest passionate parents of sublime poetry."

"The beauty of Merit is greater than the merit of Beauty.......
Once in a while, during the moon days of our travel as poets, you will meet someone who has the merits of both worlds. Such people are rare stars in the constellation of humanity. They inspire, inspire, and inspire again all of us who love beauty and truth; truth and beauty."

"The man who chases wealth with all his might chases a treacherous fire. The man who chases his passions day and night chases a most ravenous tiger. The man who chases his dreams perpetually chases winds of happiness who slips from his gaze, I'm told. But he who chases good deeds for the sake of love and the smile of mercy will find paradise lingering in his heart and heaven living in his soul."

"The small seeds that G-D plants in life become tall trees that touch the heart of heaven."

THE LAST WISH OF THE SULTAN OF LOVE

After the COVID Wars culminated with the Battle of The Ten Kings in Tribeca New York City, four rulers emerged from the putrid medical dust of dead souls that covered the city,

The Emperor of Brooklyn, The Shogun of Queens, The King of the Bronx, and the powerful Sultan of Harlem. aka THE SULTAN OF LOVE.

After having lost lower Manhattan to the Emperor of Brooklyn, the Sultan of Harlem retired to his palace in Marcus Garvey Park, with badly wounded pride. He knew that he could not survive nor could ever hope to compete in the battle to vanquish the Mansa of Staten Island (the only unscathed province in THE GREAT CITY). So, as he prepared for death, he summoned his four wives and asked which of them loved him enough to join him in the afterlife. He assured the volunteer that her family would be cared for until the end of time.

The four women ran in four directions, but he had them dragged back. The first wife, Wealth, who was the most beautiful of his wives in his eyes, demurred and said, "Oh Sultan even if they bury me with you, another man will dig me up and I will soon be his wife." True." said the Sultan; and dismissed her "I will give you to my estate." The estate accepted her.

The second beautiful wife, his Position in the world, whom he loved immensely said, "Oh Sultan of the People, as soon as you die someone will take your place on the throne. Your position will vanish like a cloud; and someone else will sit in your position. I will automatically become his wife. "True," said the Sultan, "I will give you to history." However, history refused saying, "Oh Sultan, no man can control his Position in history." The Sultan wept.

Then the third beautiful wife was summoned, his Pleasures of ten thousand nights. As he summoned her, her perfume transported him to the Kingdom of his Memories (one of the Seven Kingdoms of the Mind). Then she said "Oh Sultan, I cannot go with you. For you are going to a place where pleasure has no food, clothing, or shelter." She turned to a pillar of ice as she got closer to him. His Pleasure was frozen in time. The Sultan wept.

"Where is my fourth beautiful wife?" the Sultan bellowed. "I'm here!" cackled an old bent and frail willow of a woman, without teeth or hair. "I will go with you. No problem, Sonny Boy"

"But you are no longer beautiful. What's happened? You are my mighty Deeds which I loved! I made statutes and commissioned paintings of your beauty. Now you have no teeth, no hair, and you are bent like a willow; although we are both only 40 years old."

"I'll explain," wittingly she said. I have no teeth because you never smiled at anyone. I am frail because you never supported anyone's interest but your own. I have no hair because I wore a wig that was woven on the loom of your pride! Oh Sultan, I will be in your bed, as your wife, forever. For I am your Deeds and you cannot divorce me!" After hearing this the Sultan died of shock. He was buried and his fourth wife with him. Well, truth be told, she jumped into a coffin which was rented for the occasion.

A new Sultan OF HARLEM took the dead Sultan's place; and he loved Beauty and Truth; and he was kind to the people. He was a wise man who united The Seven Kingdoms of the Mind, within himself:

The Kingdoms of The Drives
The Five Senses
The Ego
Memories,
Reasons
The Conscience and
The Will

He established THE PEOPLES REPUBLIC OF HARLEM, which lasted for a thousand years. None of the Emperors, Shoguns, Mansas, or Kings could overtake him because he married Righteous.......
THE MOST WISE BEAUTIFUL AND INSPIRING OF WIVES

THE THREE PEARLS

I met three precious pearls on the road to Nod one night. These three sisters were Wisdom, Knowledge, and Understanding. They asked me for answers to questions about life which I did not know or understand. Humbly I pleaded, "Please instruct me." Knowledge and Understanding laughed at my naivete, but Wisdom had mercy on me; and followed me, carrying her lamp into the night. I turned my head, smiled and walked. How could I not embrace her? For her kiss enthralls my heart like the dew of the dawn. So, I married Wisdom; and now Knowledge and Understanding are my sisters-in-law. These three lamps are the lights of my life.

She gave him a cup of tea, to rid him of his fever; and wiped his brow with the hem of her cotton dress. She smiled at him; and asked him to walk with her. She told him to take a deep breath, embrace the rays of the sun. "I do this for you my son. I do this for all of you." He looked at her with great admiration and uttered, "Thank you MOTHER NATURE!"

Mother Nature

She gave him a cup of tea, to rid him of his fever; and wiped his brow with the hem of her cotton dress. She smiled at him; and asked him to walk with her. She told him to take a deep breath, embrace the rays of the sun. "I do this for you my son. I do this for all of you." He looked at her with great admiration and uttered, "Thank you *MOTHER NATURE!*"

DURING THE STORM

During the din and darkness of the storm
I shall run to the hills of you
And seek refuge in the warmth of the valley
Until peace is due
For surely peace is the offspring of love
And love flowers on heavenly hills

THE RISING DAY/THE TENDER DAWN

Morning's kiss awakens sun and flowers
Letting daffodils have their way
I rise to your touch, endowed with superpowers
To love you deeply, another day!

THE POEM OF THE TREE OF LOVE

In Fall
The tree tells the magnificent story of her life in many chapters of color
In Winter
The tree appears to be dead and all love is lost from the arms of her branches
But the tree is not dead; and love lies deep in the roots of her buried heart
She waits for Spring to come
Riding on the wings of the Eastern wind
Reciting again the poem of the cherry blossom
Ready again forever for the four seasons of life
LIFE IS A TREE
A TREE IS LIFE

THE LOVE OF MOTHER EARTH

When you were small and very pale
I fed you grapes from the sweetest dale
When you were sick and frail
I led you to herbs that could prevail
When questions flew from the nest of your heart quite blind
I wised you with parables sublime
I was always gentle and kind
All those hurricanes started in your mind
Although you quaked my heart when I was mistreated
I forgave you and prayed that you would not be deleted
Each night I covered your dreams with a silvery moon
I summoned cooling winds to be your servants at noon
I inspired poetry, song and much more than this
That dirt on your face is my inspiring kiss
I hear the tears of your kin
Your blessed sister and brother, as they tuck you in
Into my strong and gentle arms, will you remain
For eons of sun and eons of rain
For I am strong, a woman like no other
I am the earth I am your earth mother

THE TREE WHO LOVED ME

If you love a seedling or flower,
Water her everyday with tenderness.
And smile upon her with the warmth of your heart.
Then one morning when you awaken for that walk in the park,
You will hear the call of a bountiful tree singing in the rain like a lark,
Laden with the lush ripe fruit and perfume scented bark,
She will offer up her fruit and she will be joyous too
And she will truly always be the tree who fell in love with you

FIVE LOVE HAIKU

Without fire no warmth
Without lotus never spring
Without love no life.

The heart will not melt
Until Spring forgives winter
For his coldest ways

A Heart kissing peace
Meanwhile making love to war
Buries our dreams

Treasures of touch excite
Treasures of the heart delight
Fools chase Fall tigers

Wisdom opens minds
Love unlocks doors of heaven
Nightingales escape

THE HEAVENLY SEDUCTION

Every flower is a love child, Darling
It all began when the Earth surrendered her love to the Sky
And filled his clouds with the wet kisses of her passionate dreams
Then the Sky returned the kisses; and so, it rained
Yes, My love it was like this
The Earth did not resist
She surrendered to the thunder of his embrace
And now, Darling, there are flowers all over the place
But none as lovely as the exquisite beauty of your face!

She stood there upon the sandy shore, statuesque, waiting for his appearance. And then it happened, he returned to her, as he'd promised. He approached her, full of awe and admiration. For time had not diminished her beauty. He noticed her charcoal-colored hair had now evolved into a gracious shade of silvery gray. She looked at the Sun's amber departure and whispered sweetly, "I've missed you. Have you kept your promise?" "I have, My Love." He replied. She smiled and softly said, "Then let us embrace the Moon, she hastens for us." The MOON greeted the SUN; took her place in the heavens and smiled upon the waters. Their bodies now almost as close as their hearts had always been. He holds her near as they allow each wave to remind them of life's blessings.

East of the Moon &
West of the Sun

She stood there upon the sandy shore, statuesque, waiting for his appearance. And then it happened, he returned to her, as he'd promised. He approached her, full of awe and admiration. For time had not diminished her beauty. He noticed her charcoal-colored hair had now evolved into a gracious shade of silvery gray. She looked at the Sun's amber departure and whispered sweetly, "I've missed you. Have you kept your promise?" "I have, My Love." He replied. She smiled and softly said, "Then let us embrace the Moon, she hastens for us." The MOON greeted the SUN; took her place in the heavens and smiled upon the waters. Their bodies now almost as close as their hearts had always been. He holds her near as they allow each wave to remind them of life's blessings.

BY THE RETIRING DAY

By the stirring dawn
Who emerges from the satin of the night
By the staff of the declining day
Who fades into the setting western light
I, John, was born to be your brother and partner in the jubilations and tribulations of life

I, like you, emerged from the oceans of a dream
Like you, I have listened to stories from the mouths of many rivers
And I, like you, have tried to make the best of this beautiful world

By the pen, I have lived
By the mind, I have searched for the face of Wisdom
By the token of time, I have not diminished my enthusiasm
And, by the Grace of G-D, time has not diminished me

By my eyes, I have wept over the cruelty of humanity and our unfathomable insanity
By my smile, I and the music of the spheres have cheered the true beauty of the human spirit
By my heart, I have loved and the mere idea of love has loved me, in return
Love and Duty
Truth and Beauty
These things will always be intertwined
Falling in Love is wonderful
The sustaining of Duty is divine
Truth is the spouse of the heart
And Beauty, My Dear, is the soul of all art

And so, I say, "Peace and Goodnight."

And that to love peace is to stand up for right
And that to love is to want the best for the one you love (that is a must!!!)
And to want the best for your neighbor and the downtrodden soul, who sleeps in the dust!
For we are all one; and all the downtrodden are us!

MY RETURN TO NEW YORK (*From Pearls of Love Island in the Land of Nod*)

It was 12 before midnight and the streets of STAR-METROPOLIS were paved with stars. I was in love and walking in the wonderful Land of Nod, far away from maddening crowds of days in canyons of steel in THE LAND OF AWAKE. Dream trucks were plowing up and down the highways and byways of the misty night, delivering dreams to their proper human destinations. Millions of customers had logged onto the night with their minds; and dream packages were being deposited into millions of open minds, whose eyes were shut wide with wonder.

I heard lighting and thunder. It was raining on The Island of the Pearls of Love in the Land of Nod. The sweet lips of a cosmic woman was pouring kisses of passion upon the tender turquoise of my soul. I was waiting for an Imagination Bus or a Dream Taxi that might ferry me over time and space back to my home in my beloved Harlem. I had overstayed my visa in this, strange, estranged world where I had been an involuntary visitor. I saw two huge Dream Tankers (trucks labeled with caution signs) "Danger! Vehicle contain explosive nightmares!" they read. One of the huge tankers stopped in front of a porcelain house in front of 1600 Pensive Avenue and delivers liquid nightmare through a hose in the ground leading to the minds of the inhabitants of the house. I soon heard loud, frantic, other worldly screams coming from the porcelain house at 1600 Pensive Avenue. And beings with orange hair fled the houses as if chased by some hellish conflagration. The screams were so loud, in fact, that they shattered the windows of the porcelain house like a tornado breaking its way out of the prison of bottles. I started to run. I dared not panic, for panicking can lead to a recession of the spirit or a depression of the mind! Finally, I saw a happy looking Yellow Dream Bus marked "Dream express, Destination New York." I smiled and thought to myself, "This is just what I wanted!" I started to board the bus; then from out of nowhere a winged creature violently pushed me to the ground. It was The Nightingale!

The Blue Nightingale, whose cage had once held me prisoner. I thought I had escaped or paid my debt to the SOCIETY OF WRITERS. "Son of pens," the Nightingale shouted, "do not get in any vehicle on the highway or you will never, ever, return to the Land of Wakefulness in Harlem again. These vehicles are only fantasy buses. They are dream excursions. The buses without drivers are DAY-DREAMS; and the ones with drivers are NIGHT-DREAMS. Board anyone of them and you will be forever lost in the highways and byways of the Land of Nod. Follow only the Green Brick Road that shines in the moonlight of revelation; and you will find your way to the Star, who is the mother of your earth galaxy. There is a stairway between the heavens and the earth. It is called a Stairway to the Stars. This stairway is a sure way of ascent and descent. There are seven heavens and seven stairs, or steps, between each heaven. Each step that you take represents a light year of travel by light. The land of Nod is in the first heaven. You are seven steps up or seven steps down, depending on your orientation. And, please, hold onto the two handrails John, as you descend. Hold onto the hard rails of balance lest you fly off into the space of forgetfulness. Do not remove your hands from the rails of the stairs for any reason, Oh Son of Pens! You must deliver the stories, that you have, to the human press. Your stories are like grapes; they must go to the press. There is a thirsty mind waiting to drink the juice of those grapes at the end of your journey. Do you understand Son of Pens?" ordered the Blue Nightingale. "I do," I relented. "I just want to get my freedom and go home." "Farewell" the nightingale said as she smiled at me and handed me a key. "This is the key to your cage. You are just like the other writers. You have caged yourself by your own thinking. Now free yourself, Son of Pens!" the blue nightingale laughed as she flew away.

I walked until I reached the edge of Nod; which overlooks the edge of the Star Metropolis, where the Peoples Republic of Harlem overlooks a TRISTAR BRIDGE. There, at the foot of the bridge, Green Brick Road was sandwiched between a Golden-yellow Brick Road and a blue DREAM Brick Road. I followed the GREEN BRICK ROAD to a frozen lake. When I reached the lake, a green bridge arose from under the freezing waters. I crossed the green bridge and walked 30 kilometers, till I beheld a lake of smokeless fire. The Green Brick Road ascended over the lake of fire. At the end of the lake of fire, I beheld a stairway descending. It was well lit by the light from the stars. It was a narrow stairway that descended into a black abyss.

Far beneath me, at the bottom of the stars, a thousand years away, I saw the earth the size of a golf ball turning and swirling like a slow spinning top. "Wow!" I gasped. "I am so far away from home. For a moment, I imagined myself playing the soprano saxophone at a place in Harlem called "449LA". My children and grandchildren were all there. The one I love was sitting in the audience nodding with her poignant smile, that seemed near and far away at the same time. Then **it** all faded to black. First, my saxophone became dark and silent. Then, the piano keys turned into all black keys. The bassist stopped his heart thrumming pulse and the drummer's heart beating rhythm faded into long high pitch tones, similar to that of a heart monitor attached to the failed heart of a dead man. I had to get home! My world in the Land of Wakefulness was surely dying. I grabbed the two rails tightly on both sides, as I descended into the abyss of time and space of a triple dark night. There were stars all around me. Stars to the left. Stars to the right. Stars had my back and stars stared me in the face, as I made my decent downward from the Land of Nod. A land of dreams, that hovers above the earth, beyond the 5th dimension and the 7th syllable of the universe.

In a few moments it seems I had descended 2,000 years, with just two carefully placed steps. Suddenly I was startled by an army of assassins who started ascending the stairs, "Seize him!" shouted the leader. "Seize him, kill him, and stop him. These stories of love must not reach human minds! The leader shouted, "Kill him in his sleep!" I became afraid as I saw the assassins ascending the stairs to meet me. I drew my pen from my sheath and suddenly my pen became a sword. I struck off the head of the first assassin as he reached me as he was about to pierce my abdomen with his blade. I fought the remaining assassins with skills that I had never known. The remaining assassins fled before my mighty sword pen. I proceeded down to the fourth steps of the stairway to the stars. On the fourth step, I was met by five giants. Each having one giant eye in the middle of his forehead and one in the back of his head. "Bow your five senses to us!" the leader ordered, "And we let you go home!" "I cannot!" I insisted. "My five senses belong to me; and I will bow to no one but the One who gave them to me!" "Then we will make you blind, deaf, and dumb" the leader of the five responded. Once again, I drew my pen swiftly and wrote the word "sleep," on the blackboard of the night sky. The five giants fell asleep. I stepped over them and proceeded to the next step downward. The five giants snored so loud that the very heavens seemed to shake from their snoring.

Finally, I descended to the bottom step; and there I met the most beautiful woman I had ever encountered in Nod or anywhere else in the universe even in my dreams. "John," she whispered, "I have been waiting for you." She caressed my face with the palms of her soft hands. I felt myself melting into her perfume. "No." I whispered. "Why not?" she whispered back. "Because." I whispered 'Because. Because." . "Because what?" she sighed. "I know you love me." "No, I do not." I challenged. "But you want me near you. Don't you?" the beautiful woman retorted. "Yes," I replied, "but only in my dream." "You fool!!!" the woman screamed. "Dreams cannot feed me! Silly man! You have destroyed me. How could you want me only in a dream? You, foolish, foolish, foolish, man!!!" she screamed. At that moment, two strong red monsters pulled the woman off of my chest and dragged her to a cage marked "dreams". The woman cried and laughed hysterically "You fool! You will dream about me and eventually I will be free. And I am coming to the Land of Awake to devour you! I will destroy you!" she screamed. "How dear to relegate me to a dream! I will destroy you with my beauty!" I rose to my feet and brushed off the star dust she'd left on my shoulders and sleeves.

I had one more step to take before reaching the Land of Awake. I did not know what other challenges awaited me. Then a messenger, a winged creature, came to me and spoke in the night. "John is there anything you want to tell your loved ones and readers before you take your final step down in the Land of Wakefulness? This is a step few have survived. Most travelers die in their sleep." "Say to the one I love, if you find her, and my family I am returning home to consciousness. Keep the light on for me; I hope you will be there when I get home. I am John your brother and partner in jubilation, tribulation and expectation." Just then I realized I had taken my hands off the handrails. Not once but at least three times. Then I swooned and fell. I lost my grip on the two rails. Down, down, down I went, whirling in a black space. Down I went into a vortex of whirling confusion. I saw the earth spinning as I crashed toward it, at such a speed that it felt as if my flesh were being peeled from my body. Then suddenly, all around me became white. Oh, what a night, it was snowing in the Land of Awakeness. I was going to crash! The snow felt like bullets or a thousand flung kung fu knives as they hit my face and body at flashing speed.

It was the month of February. It was a month I will never forget. My memory acted as a parachute, as it tremendously slowed down my descent until fell gently on a snowbank on 125th street between Frederick Douglass Blvd and Adam Clayton Powell Blvd. I was in old Harlem, in good ole New York. I could see the Apollo Theater, still lit up like a candle in the night. I could see the exquisitely sculpted statue of Harriet Tubman dancing with the elegant statue of Adam Clayton Powell. They seemed to be in love with each other. Harriet Tubman was singing (but I never knew her to be a singer). The statue of Frederic Douglass was watching jealously, waiting for the next dance. Then I awakened and found myself lying in the same drift of snow. All New York was silent, eerily silent.

It was almost 5 o'clock in the morning and there was no one on the street, but me. The sun had just opened one eye. Dawn yawned and carefully gathered her blue robe. A police car pulled up beside me with its lights flashing like some UFO from outer space. The officer yelled at me "Hey Bud! You are not allowed on the street until 6am!" "Why?" I responded. "There is a Civil War!" the officer responded. "What Civil War?" I responded. "The Civil War ended in 1865; and it ended slavery." "No kidding, you rag head! There is a war against civility. Now get into the car!" he shouted using the N word. "What year is this?" I asked.

"It's the year of the BOT." was his response as he showed me his titanium metal hands. "You saggins always violated the curfew." "But I was in Nod!" I challenged. "That's what all you 'BLACK LIVES MATTER' people claim. Lock this saggin up!" a white shirted police officer ordered, who pulled up in a second police car "He has violated the curfew!" My cell door slammed shut. Some things never change! I was in jail for violating a curfew I did not know about. How can I explain to a judge that I was in the land of Nod and could not have known about a curfew?

I could see the lieutenant's desk from my jail cell, in the 28th precinct of Harlem. Over his left side hung a cage. I could not see inside the cage, but I could hear the singing of a nightingale. A nightingale sang, "Somewhere in the night! Somewhere in the night! I could hear a nightingale sing in Harlem square." Eventually, I ended up being placed in the psych ward of NEW HARLEM HOSPITAL and was diagnosed with the disease of "Being in Love". One of the medics said it was the side effect of the ancient Covid pandemic (which is now considered a curable extinct disease). My G-D, what has this world come to?

No matter what comes to me from the nether world or above, I think that I shall ever be a witness and a citizen of love.

THE EPILOGUE OF MY SOUL

By the night and by the song of my darling's arms
By the moon and the stars who dance seamlessly together
I John fell asleep one night
When an angel left open heaven's door

That night it rained in the ocean and I wept in my dreams
I was disoriented and lost for a while, it seems
My soul had left the bed
And my body was torn from the sweet embrace of my perfumed companion
I hoped that she would wait

A poet might be called to write anytime in the emergency of the night.
Yes, I know every human born is a living, breathing, loving poem from G-d
But for me, a poet, I was a lost poem
A lost mind

I had awakened in another world somewhere
In the great somewhere
I was in a world only reachable by opened inner eyes
I tried in vain to find the long road back leading to my bed

But I kept ascending, up toward
Upward, into the realm of a Greater Somewhere
I kept ascending
I was ascending to a place I know not where or when I would stop.

The winsome melody of the flute of the night grabbed my ears

And seduced my soul into an eerie calm
I could not see but I knew
The turquoise of my soul would meet a most unusual encounter on the other side of midnight.

Still, I was rising. Still, I rose.
Upward, Upward, as if swept up into the cosmos by a hungry space-born vortex
Finally, the Flute of the Night saved me
Dragging me away into some semblance of sanity.

A somewhere surrounded by trees
Above the sedative of the mystic flute of the night, I heard nerve-fraying buzzing.
A buzzing that came nearer and nearer. It sounded like a Bee.
A Bee buzzing in my ear
A Bee buzzing in my brain
A Bee buzzing in the soul…Buzzing in my being

Suddenly it stung me,
Not once, not twice, but thrice.
The rascal savaged my flesh with its steel stinger
And like a microscopic jackhammer, it attacked me again and again.

I ran through the Street of Dreams until I reached the FOREST OF FEELINGS
I knew I was called upon to deliver another poem or book from the womb of the pregnant night
If love is born alive, I will write again
INSHALLAH

Index

(Listings in Alphabetical Order by Category, then Type, then Title)

Art

Poems

Desire

Poems

East of the Moon and West of the Sun

Home

Life

Mother Nature

Music

Poems

Passion

Poems

Stoems

Romance

Poems

Stoems

Unconditional Love

Poems

Unrequited Love

Poems

Stoems

Wisdom

Poems

Proverbs

Stoems

Index

(Listed by Title in Alphabetical Order)

Mother: A Love Like None Other
My Secret Love
Of Love, Beggars, and Wisdom
Of Poetry and Women
On the Relationship Between Mind and Heart
On the Relationship Between Wealth and Love
On the Running of Hearts and Rivers
Once
Poem for a Beautiful Friendship
Riding High
Say: Jazz Ain't Nothing But Love
Serendipity
Speak Love, Dear
The Brief Encounter
The Coltrane Ride
The Consequence of a Smile
The Dance
The Dimensions of the Heart I
The Dimensions of the Heart II
The Epilogue of My Soul
The Falling Leaves
The Four Seasons of Love
The Heavenly Seduction
The Hurricane and the Volcano
The Immigrant
The Impossible Pursuit
The Lesson
The Love of Mother Earth
The Mansions of the Heart
The Memories of a Musician

Love Potion #45
My Return to New York from Pearls of Love Island in the Land of Nod
Suicide Note from A Parker Ball Point Pen
The Allegory of the Cage
The Attraction
The Cell: A Love Story
The Cosmology of Love
The Island of Marriage
The Last Wish of the Sultan of Love
The Legend of the Lily and the Butterfly
The Mango and the Cactus
The Mighty Wall Who Fell in Love
The Pearl of Love
The Riddle of the "A" Train of Thought
The Rose and the Stone
The Ruby and the Pearl
The Ruby and the Pearl (The Second Journey)

Index

(Listed by First Line in Alphabetical Order)

"During the din and darkness of the storm, I shall run to the hills of you…"
During the Storm

"Every flower is a love child, Darling…"
The Heavenly Seduction

"I admire you deeply…"
Unrequited Love I

"I am desire…"
Desire

"I discovered you…"
Discovery

"I fell for you as a lonely tree falls on the forest ground…"
The Silent Fall

"I heard your perfume…"
The Perfumed Kiss

"I met you, you stayed…"
Serendipity

"I never knew, darling, that you loved me…"
Unspoken Love

"I saw you standing there…"
The Brief Encounter

"I was a hurricane, in a hurry to discover the meaning of my existence…"
The Hurricane and the Volcano

"I was a jazz-head, "Chasin' the Trane"…"
The Coltrane Ride

"I was a musician…"
The Memories of a Musician

"If a rich man traded his riches for love…"
On the Relationship Between Wealth and Love

"If I had searched for you among the stars…"
The Search

"If you agree to be my ocean…"
Captured

"If you are free and solvent…"
Advice to A Son II

"If you love a flower, water it gently; and keep it far away from the storm…"
Advice to A Son I

"If you love a seedling or flower, water her everyday with tenderness…"
The Tree Who Loved Me

"If you were a train, I'd ride you to last stop…"
Riding High

"In fall, the tree tells the magnificent story of her life in many chapters of color…"
The Poem of the Tree of Love

"In Spring, my love was like a tropic bull…"
The Four Seasons of Love

"In the pulsating poignant world of Jazz…"
Say: Jazz Ain't Nothing, But Love

"In this world where good and evil dwell…"
To Veterans in the Valley When the Mountains Are Not Enough

"Is it the happiness that I drink when I look into your eyes…"
What Makes Me Love You?

"It's Autumn, I behold its voluptuous red and gold sprinkled smile…"
A Day in the Life of a Heart

"Lips thrill the night…"
The Lesson

"Love is not given…"
Love is not Free

"Love is work…"
Advice to A Son-In-Law

"Many will swear by the sun that the poetry of a woman lies in the sublime…"
Of Poetry and Women

"Men run like cool rivers to the warm oceans of women…"
On the Running of Hearts and Rivers

"Morning's kiss awakens sun and flowers…"
The Rising Day/The Tender Dawn

"Of course, I care…"
Poem for A Beautiful Friendship

"Oh, my love…"
The Mansions of the Heart

"Once I was a proud romantic guy…"
Holidays Can Really Hang You Up the Most

"Once upon a time I lived…"
Once (YOLO YO-LOVED)

"Once upon a time, the sky fell in love with the sea…"
The Sky and the Sea

"Pour me a glass of your love…"
A Glass of Love, Please

"Say what passion can knock down the mountains…"
The Multiplication and Art of Love

"Some love is born from the fire of unrelenting passion…"
Mother: A Love Like None Other

"Sweetheart, you are my one and only flame…"
The Song of the Candle and the Flame

"The dimensions of the heart cannot be measured…all creation comes from love…"
The Dimensions of the Heart II

"The dimensions of the heart cannot be measured…the touch between you and I…"
The Dimensions of the Heart I

"The face of love is indeed one of a kind…"
The Seven Gifts of Love

"The first time that I heard your voice on the phone…"
A Prisoner of Love

"The leaves fall like red teardrops from the blue rain drenched branches of October…"
The Falling Leaves

"The mind seeks to always know…"
Five Short Morning Poems

"The small seeds that G-D plants in life become tall trees that touch the heart of heaven…"
Just Coffee

"The sun cannot stay…"
The Impossible Pursuit

"The sun is jealous of your kiss…"
Love Tempest in Heaven

"The time to speak love soon disappears…"
Speak Love, Dear

"The words, "I love you," made the stars…"
"I Love You"

"There was a man who lost his legs…"
Of Love, Beggars, and Wisdom

"To break through a stone…"
Love Mountain and the Rose

"What would I give to see you…"
What Would I Give?

"What would I give to see you…"
Unrequited Love II

"When the sun closes his eyes; and the world is dark…"
I Will Be There

"When you were small and very pale, I fed you grapes from the sweetest dale…"
The Love of Mother Earth

"Who will separate a pearl from its luster…"
On the Relationship Between Mind and Heart

"Wisdom is a late bloomer…"
The Wife of Life

"Without fire, no warmth…"
Five Love Haiku

"You are Spring…"
Joy

"You never said that you love me…"
The Voice of the Heart

"You rule the dimensions of the night…"
The Pursuit

"You were there, in Autumn air…"
The Consequence of a Smile

"Your touch healed my heart…"
The Touch

Proverbs
"Better to conquer a heart than vanish a city…"
Forgotten Proverbs

"The building of a love relationship between a man and woman is like the building…"
The Tower of Relationships

Stoems
"After the COVID wars culminated with the Battle of the Ten Kings in Tribeca, New York City, …"
The Last Wish of the Sultan of Love

"Apple tree! Apple tree! How many leaves are in your hair?…"
A Blossom Is A Promise

"By the token of time, men begin as brothers of the cage; only a few escape the rage of ignorance…"
The Allegory of the Cage

"Dear John, Once upon a time, you loved me…"
Suicide Note from A Parker Ball Point Pen

"He dashed eagerly toward dawn. The war was over…"
Crocus: The Tao Of Two Snow Flowers

"Heaven always keeps astride its mystic gate, but sometimes those who love must wait…"
I Waited for You

"I closed my face with my hands…"
The Cell: A Love Story

"I recently hospitalized because I was afflicted with a case of love insanity."
Love Insanity

"I took a long road back to myself after my love insanity fling…"
Love Potion #45

"It was 12 before midnight; and the streets of Star-Metropolis were paved with stars…"
My Return To New York From Pearls Of Love Island In The Land of Nod

"Once I was a Prince; and I was married to five women…"
The Island of Marriage

"Once upon a rhyme, there was no past, present, or future…"
A Time for Love

"One night without moon, without stars…"
The Pearls of Love

"Planted seeds of knowledge, in the heavens and earth, and in ourselves…"
The Cosmology of Love

"Stand tall against the wind. Do not weep because you have lost something…"
The Legend of the Lily and the Butterfly

"The rose and the stone, eternal symbols of love and fidelity…"
The Rose and the Stone

"There are seven walls in the mountains of the mind and seven gates to heaven divine…"
The Mighty Wall Who Fell in Love

"There is a river between life and death; and every man must cross the water of his deeds…"
The Riddle of the "A" Train of Thought

"There was once a mango tree who was blessed to give birth to the sweetest, juiciest, most perfect fruit for a thousand summers…"
The Mango and The Cactus

"There was once a Ruby in the mountain of love that desired a Pearl…"
The Ruby and the Pearl

"Through the ages and in the books of sages, the mind and heart are inseparable…"
The Ruby and the Pearl (The Second Journey)

"When she first laid eyes on him, the shock and warmth of his smile lit a raging fireplace in her heart…"
The Attraction

THE FIVE PAIRS OF SHOES

Dr. John "Satchmo" Mannan

THE FIVE PAIRS OF SHOES

"If the tongues of shoes could speak, they would warn the foolish and reprise the wisdom of the wise." – **Dr. John S. Mannan**

"Time rhymes with reason in the parallel Universe of Nod." – **Dr. John S. Mannan**

Once upon a rhyme in the Land of Nod, a young man was stolen from the continent of Mubassa Land as he played in the sugar cane fields of Afrolonia. His name was Uhuru, which, in his native tongue, means freedom. He was chained to the bottom of a rickety wooden ship named *Cassa Dolorosa* with 499 other captives; and forced to cross the Sea of Blood. During the passage, many of his fellow captives died in the depths of despair. Some jumped into the Sea of Blood, others died in a desperately unfair fight with their captors, who carried magic weapons that could freeze a man's brain in seconds.

Uhuru survived the passage; and when they landed, he was sold to an evil planter in Westlandia. The evil planter lived in a big white house and owned 400 acres of black cotton fields. Black cotton, like black wool, was rare. It was extremely coveted because it could be spun to make valuable black cloth. Also, many considered black cloth magical.

Upon arrival, Uhuru was whipped within five inches of his life as part of his initiation into slavery. Next, he was taken to a cave dwelling tucked in the side of a mystic mountain where dwelled the Evil Cobbler of Mis-candor.

"Make shoes for my slave," ordered the Evil Planter, "so that he will never be able to run away from my plantation or stray from what I will teach him." "Ah," said the Evil Cobbler, "I have a pair just his size. These shoes are called 'Saggins.' I will screw them into his feet and he'll never be able to move more than 600 feet beyond the boundaries of the plantation. What do you call this slave?" "I call him 'Idiot', the Evil Planter said, "which is Greek for nigger." Both The Evil Planter and Evil Cobbler laughed heartily.

"I am Uhuru," interrupted the angry young man, "which means freedom." The Evil Cobbler and the Evil Planter, upon hearing the pride in Uhuru's voice, beat him within four inches of his life. After which, the 'Saggin' shoes were screwed into his feet.

"Saggins are for Niggas," the Evil Cobbler spued with and evil laugh.

At this point, Uhuru felt defeated. As time went by and he wore the "Saggins," his mind began to change. He began to hate himself and hate his condition. Nevertheless, he resolved to fight for his freedom by any means possible. Night after night he would gaze at the shoes on his feet and think about how he could free himself from them. Finally, one night he figured it out and, with all the strength he could muster, cut away the shoes and escaped the plantation.

However, the area around the plantation was mined with anti-escape thorns that tore his bare feet with each step. So, he needed help.

He made it somehow to Evil Mountain, where he seized the Evil Cobbler in his sleep. He tied him up by his feet and rained blows upon his back with a birch tree stick. "Stop! Do not hit me again," cried the Evil Cobbler. "I will do whatever you want!" "Make me some freedom shoes," Uhuru demanded firmly. "Right away," cried the Evil Cobbler. He immediately began to make the shoes from yellow cow's skin and called them "Coloreds" shoes. Uhuru put on his "colored" shoes and took flight.

He found his way out of the area into a town called Crowsville. There he saw signs that read "Whites Only" and "Colored Only" everywhere. He walked down a street he and stopped in front of a restaurant that had a sign saying, "Only White People Here, Nigger Don't You Dare." "What is a nigger?" he wondered. He remembered being called that daily by the Evil Planter.

As he stood in front of the restaurant, from which sumptuous smells filled the air, he cast his shadow upon the door. Suddenly, from every direction, armed guards and the Honky-Tonk Police aggressively approached him and beat him within three inches of his life. "You colored people must know your place!" said the rogue officers. He was taken back to the Evil Planter, who wasted no time; and proceeded to beat him within two inches of his life. This time the Evil Planter confined Uhuru to the house, where he could watch him closely. Nevertheless, after some time, Uhuru managed to escape again.

He trekked back to Evil Mountain to confront the Evil Cobbler. Uhuru demanded, "Make me some freedom shoes! And don't even think about tricking me!" "Right away," shuddered the Evil Cobbler as Uhuru seized his red beard. The Evil Cobbler immediately made Uhuru a new, third pair of shoes to walk in, which were called "Negros." As he gave Uhuru the shoes he said, "You will be comfortable in your new identity." Uhuru slipped into the shoes and left Evil Mountain with deliberate and determined speed. Suddenly, his thinking began to change.

This time, when he arrived in Crowsville, he saw Black and Brown people gathered together in front of the white restaurant. They were chanting, "We shall overcome." Within minutes, though, the Honky-Tonk

Police and armed guards descended upon the black and brown people with dogs, hoses and thick hickory sticks. They broke bones and savagely slashed black and brown skins. Uhuru was amongst them. He suffered the same brutality as the others who were gathered and were placed in a prison called La Selva.

Despite imprisonment, the ever-clever, Uhuru escaped through seven gates and trekked back to the Evil Cobbler's lair, hidden in the cave of Evil Mountain. When Uhuru arrived, he found the Evil Cobbler trying to escape from Evil Mountain. Uhuru grabbed him and hung him upside down as he yelled, "You will deceive me no longer! I know where the power lies. It lies within shoes and their soles/souls. Where is your black leather that will match my skin?" Uhuru demanded. For I am Black like the skin of the sun; and the light inside of me must be brighter than a thousand nights filled with stars. My spirit walks on stars more numerous than all the grains of sand on this earth. If little grains of sands are free to travel in the wind, then I must be a free man in this world! You, Evil Cobbler and your friend The Evil Planter will never deny me the discovery of my dignity and distinction."

The, now trembling, Evil Cobbler refused to speak. Uhuru began to strike the Evil Cobbler and tear off his red shoes. "No, no, no," cried the cobbler, "you will destroy my power! The Black leather is under the Anvil of Thunder," he reluctantly confessed as he pointed to a large anvil in the rear of the shop.

Nevertheless, Uhuru forcibly removed the Evil Cobbler's shoes; and the cobbler, who was already a midget, began to shrink and shrink until he was the size of a medicine ball. Suddenly the sphere shaped Evil Cobbler was transformed into a small white snake. Uhuru seized the snake by its hideous head, stuffed it in a red clay pot, and covered the pot with three clay covers. He then buried it beneath a plot of barren bitter earth where no one would find it. "May you be bound here for a thousand years!" Uhuru proclaimed with a sense of relief and empowerment.

Now that Uhuru was given the liberating material, he began to make pairs of Black shoes with the Black leather. When he tried on the first pair of the black shoes he had made, he immediately felt great strength flow through his body. An overwhelming sense of pride flowed through his entire being. With the intention of helping others, he worked tirelessly to make 30 pairs of Black shoes in as many days. Then, one night he travelled back to the old plantation with the 30 pair of these powerful Black shoes. He slipped into their living quarters and excitedly announced, "Put on these Black shoes and feel the freedom you've never known!" As soon as the enslaved descendants put on the Black shoes they began to chant "What time is is?......It's the hour for Black Power!" And from that day forward they knew that Black lives would matter.

The chants of the people were so loud and powerful that it could be heard as far as The Big White House. This sudden acceptance of empowerment caused fear to explode in the heart of The Evil Planter. He sent an overseer to town to alert the Honky-Tonk police; and soon the police arrived with their brain-freezing ice guns loaded.

"Take off those Black power shoes…" they yelled, "…or we will freeze your brains with misinformation, shoot you full of bulletins, and beat you within an inch of your lives!" "No way…" replied the ex-slaves; "…now is the hour of Black Power, we know who you are and what you have stolen from us.

Uhuru then grabbed the Evil Planter and demanded, "Drop your freeze weapons or the Evil Planter suffer!" Before the Honkey-Tonk police could respond, the Evil Planter desperately yelled, "You fools! Do whatever he says! Remember, my Black cotton pays your salaries!" The Honkey-Tonk police complied and immediately dropped their weapons. Uhuru then ordered, "All of you Honkey-Tonk soldier boys, TAKE OFF YOUR SHOES!" The Evil Planter nervously interjected, "Just do what he says!" The Honkey-Tonk police, although confused, promptly complied reluctantly removing their shoes, and began to shiver. Uhuru proudly proclaimed to the recently liberated people, "There's no need to fear, my Brothers and Sisters. For our oppressors are now powerless without their shoes of oppression. Uhuru then turned to remove the Evil Planters's shoes. The Evil Planter pleaded, "Please don't take off my shoes. You will take away all of my dignity and power." Uhuru replied, "You may keep your illusion of dignity and power. As long as you stay in that White House; and never leave. You are confined for the rest of your days to the illusion that you have created." The Evil Planter sadly promised, "I promise….I promise, I will never leave!" Uhuru replied, "Rest assure, we will be watching over you and our freedom."

Uhuru instructed his newly liberated comrades to collect the shoes of supremacy worn by the Honkey-Tonk police. After which, they ceremoniously burned the shoes in a bonfire of vanities. Then Uhuru admonished, "There will be no recriminations or revenge. Treat all men fairly; and fight only against those who fight against you or the freedom of others."

So, it came to pass that Uhuru and the ex-slaves of the Big White House became freed men and regained their lost identity.

Later in time, on the recommendation of Uhuru, the ex-slaves changed their shoes for Transparent ones. The Transparent shoes became a fashion fixture amongst the youth and the elders, everywhere. These Transparent shoes revealed the true soles/souls of men; and finally became the style of all times. The identity of all people (White, Black, Red, and Yellow) became a united identity. Human is the true identity of all men. Everything else is the pretentious clothing of culture woven on the looms and the experiences of living in the mountains, plains, forests, jungles, savannahs, seashores, icy plateaus, and deserts.

The **liberated ex-slaves**, now free "at last", began to open stores and trade with all men. The town's name of Crowsville was change to Uhuru Village or Villa de Libertad. And all honest men prospered therein.

The Evil Planter died still wearing his false shoes of White supremacy. He refused to change and his feet had become gangrenous while other parts of him transformed into the porcelain white of a pernicious leprosy. And so, he died of his obtusely false pride.....Death, the wily hunter, always follows the scent of hubris.

Everything must change in time. Injustice becomes justice if you strive for it. Slavery becomes freedom if you fight for it. Ignorance becomes knowledge, wisdom and understanding if you strive for it. The fruits of the tree of life which grow within the gardens of the self also grow in the gardens of the earthly order and in the gardens of heavenly stars.

No man is ever far from his true humanity. Remove the artificial shoes of this world and stand upon the soles/souls of love and our common humanity. All else are the shoes of vanity worn upon the path of insanity.

Note To The Reader

Why I wrote, "The Five Pairs of Shoes"...

What I have written about in the story of the five pairs of shoes underpins three essential, but spectacularly hidden truths.

The first is that mentality underpins all things in our material and metaphysical worlds. The Creator or Divine mind gave the universe a paradigm of pairs. All things have parents. The father is the idea/concept and the mother (or matrix) is the design that gives birth to the concept.

This truth gives birth to a second truth which is that man means mentality. Man is not just a collection of bones, sinew, and blood but a type of mentality or designed mind. Man, then, means mind or mentality; and any man is what he thinks what he perceives and what he believes.

The third truth encompasses the true nature of the history of slavery and freedom. It simply says that if man means mind, he who controls the mind controls man. Within this construct of dominance, physical plantations and physical slavery can be abolished by law or custom. Mental plantations can exist whereby people laboring under false concepts become the slaves of ideas created to destroy their true identity as human beings.

Freedom is the process of throwing off the clothing of enslaving concepts of what it is to be a human being.

The identity of human beings or Homo Sapiens *(thinking beings)* is derived from the matrix of our experiences in the universe of the mind. This mental universe (after hosting a process similar to making rain) distills upon us our unique sense of self as human beings. Discovering the wondrous and winsome state called our "humanity" is like discovering a garden of delight in a desert of mundane materiality. We achieve by this discovery the ability to identify each other by the color of our ideas and the content of our character, instead of by the incidental garments of our outward appearances. Such a discovery is accomplished only by unbiased searching, critical dialogue, and the epiphany from the mutual sharing of truth. Nevertheless, there will always be obstacles to this process.

Children, when they are born do not know that they are human (nor do lion cubs know that they are lions). It even takes time for children to realize that their own hands belong to them.

Some things must be learned by experience and experimentation, but the rest of a human's identity is taught by the social order (i.e., by biological parents and the surrogate mothers of school matriculation systems called alma mater/soul mother) and by the child's mother tongue, which paints the world in the parochial colors and palpable concepts, of social customs and belief.

As a result of the above process, people identify themselves by their languages or mother tongues, by the land in which they are born or sometimes by a common belief system or ancestry. When people are taken away from the land of their birth (or from the memory of that land), forced to speak a new language for generations, and told they are not human beings they have been de facto dehumanized (which is a crime against all humanity).

These unfortunate dehumanized victims will become identified by the cultural shoes(roles) that they are forced to wear as they walk along the backways and byways assigned to them in a stratified social order.

Only the love of freedom and faith in a Supreme Beneficent Power can help *"mis-shoed"* human beings recapture the paradise lost of human dignity, distinction, and integrity.

The story of "The Five Pairs of Shoes" is a story about history and about the love of freedom that beats in the heart of every Homo Sapien.

It is a love supreme!

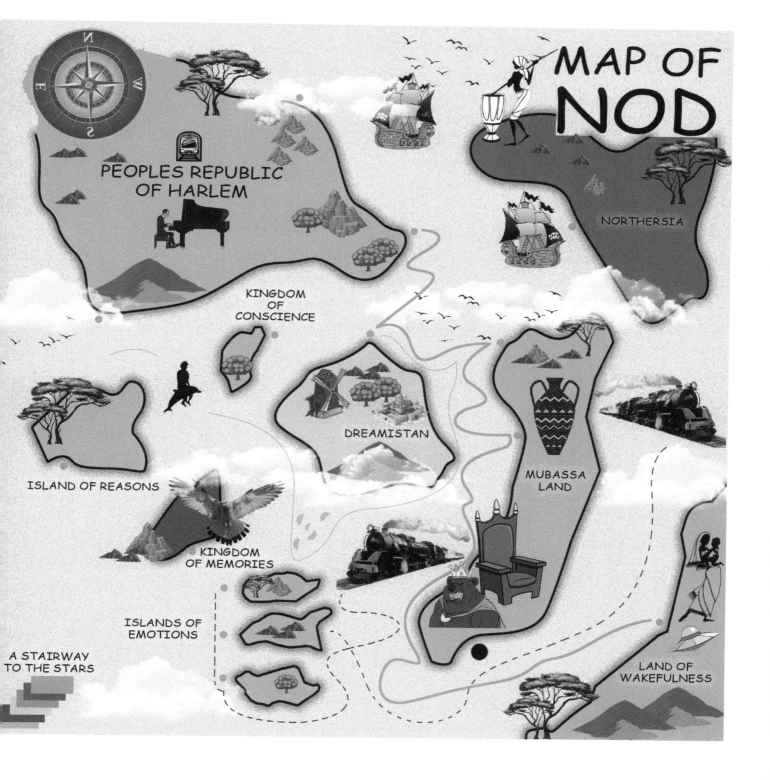

Love comes from above and descends like rain upon the flower of the human heart. And from my heart to the CREATOR flows these words....

Creator

L ove comes from above and descends like rain upon the flower of the human heart. And from my heart to the CREATOR flows these words....

OF AQUARIUMS, OCEANS, AND LOVE

The world is an aquarium; and we are fish swimming in it
Striving against the natural and artificial currents of our existence
Our Owner feeds us and cares for us
Keeping our environment balanced
He places a light over the cover and a cover over the light
Our minds only see shadows beyond the vast shining glass
We fish, in the aquarium of life, fall in love
Mistaking a small lamp for the moon above
So soon one by one, we are fished out of the aquarium world
And released in the ocean of eternity
Then beyond the glass we see
We sigh. We cry. We see.
Ah, such is life! Ah, such is love! Ah such was me!

PRAISE BE TO THE CREATOR

Praise be to the CREATOR, who is love
Who placed the flame of love in all living things
In this way, the very stars of the night become lamps to our mystic feet
These are the Pearls of Love that descended into my pen
As I beheld the eyes of love in the night
These are the Pearl of Love that I borrowed from the song of a rose
That grew by the sea
That I gathered from the plantations of the wind
Where my scattered thoughts labored to find true meaning within
These are the pearls of a poor man
Who always begs the book of heaven for greater meaning

These are Pearls of Love gleaming in the sun,
Free as her light…Free as a song…Free for everyone

THE RHAPSODY: THE ACKNOWLEDGMENT OF LOVE AND KNOWLEDGE

With the name of the Beneficent and Merciful Creator
By the morning sun
By the gift of The Dawn
By the evening star
And his beloved spouse The Night
I John bear witness to the mercies of heaven
And to the mystery of the two gifts:
Knowledge and Love

A SONG OF LOVE AND PRAISE TO MY LORD THE CREATOR MOST BENEFICENT MOST BEAUTIFUL

Praise belongs to G-D, the Greatest. His Majesty and His Beauty are united and unlimited. His proximity to the heart is nearer than a lamp is to its own light. His loftiness is too large to be overtaken by any explanation, expressed. or implied. His essence is too sublime to be limited and described by any poet's pen or any explanation of a scientist or a scribe. It is beyond any distance, any physical or spiritual descent or ascent, or the enthronement of anything upon a throne.

He has no need or haste to seek an object because all wonderful things even death are His creation; and they belong to Him. By His grace, the created things that He has made enjoy and bathe in His Mercy.

He is the Author of the satisfaction and it is we creatures who gain some satisfaction by way of love and the possession of love or by the reuniting with something or someone who has been missed.

He is The Observer. The Power. The Splendor. The Grandeur. The Magnificence is His.

HIS essence is beyond any resemblance to any other essences. LOVE is His gift and the most often unopened present. By the lamp of the luster in your eyes I see heaven. By the touch of your hand, I am tailored in the garments of paradise. By the Nirvana of your kiss, I drink of four rivers.......

A river of milk

A river of wine

A river of sparkling water

A river of honey divine

A foretaste of things abundant in a world UP ABOVE. By the token of time a mercy from my Lord WHO IS AND GIVES LOVE.

LOVE HIDDEN...LOVE REFINED...LOVE UNLIMITED...LOVE DIVINE

ABOUT THE AUTHOR

Dr. John "Satchmo" Mannan is the *nom de plume* (penname), if you will, of Dr. Mujib Mannan retired Professor of the American Experience Law, Literature and History at the College of New Rochelle, University of the Virgin Islands and other university venues for nearly 30 years. Dr. Mannan, as a person, is interested in the entire 360 degrees of life beyond his doctorate and graduate degrees in jurisprudence, history, etc. The author is an educator, lawyer, historian, poet, short storyteller, essayist, jazz musician, marketing consultant and executive director of an affordable housing initiative in Harlem.

Born in Harlem, the author has written several books, including *"Cultural Imperialism," "The History of the Harlem Mosque," "The Legend of Lute," "Tales of the Nightingale," "The Arabic Words in the English Language," "The Rubiyat of Abdul Mannan,"* etc.

His poetry is in several anthologies, but under an earlier nom de plume John McRae. These poems include *"Ghetto 68," "We Be Word Sorcerers," "Three Hundred Sixty Degrees of Blackness,"* etc. Other venues such as the African Sun Times, Living City, The Thinker have published his work under the name Mujib Mannan. His *"Peace Haiku Collection"* has been chosen for inclusion in the city of Philadelphia "Peace Project."

In 2016, Aladdin Books International published his collection of short stories called: *"Mubassa's Dream"* and *"18 Legends from The Land of Nod"*. This book geared for all ages (8to 98) was a tonic for the human imagination while it tackled moral and sociopolitical issues while using myth and allegorical tool of a bedtime story.

This book, THE PEARLS OF LOVE was written during the COVID19 pandemic. It's a book of poems and short stories about the passions, dimensions, importance, and majesty of love in our human lives. "From passion to compassion to rhapsody, life begins with love," Mannan says. "And we hope that it ends with a testimony of angels that we have loved correctly, that we have loved mercy and justice and wives and children (all children) and life and learning and positive community development." "Life," he continues, "poses its ultimate, truth and paradoxes in the form of questions that cause the reader to think and ultimately confess the true beauty and wonder of the creation and the human spirit. But ultimately our lives are weighed on the scale of what and whom we have loved or failed to love and how we have loved." This discovery and awareness of the divine in the act of loving is the beginning of a wisdom that assists the individual and social man on the journey toward felicity. dignity and distinction.

In 2018, he was an International Jazz Day Awardee for his contribution to jazz and during the same year he was a featured performing artist at Carnegie Hall's, *"A Gathering of Eagles."* His Jazz CD, *"Ten O'clock Jazz"* was released December 14, 2014, by New Savoy Records

He has received several civic awards for community service including a NY City Council Citation as An Outstanding New Yorker by Miguel Martinez and a New York Senate Recognition Award Feb 5, 2021, for community service.

The author's many interests and skills have enriched his human experience and the lives of those around him.

• • •